MURDER

ON THE WEST COAST

Irish detectives investigate
a bungled kidnapping

DAVID PEARSON

Paperback edition published by

The Book Folks

London, 2018

ISBN 978-1-9829-6736-9

www.thebookfolks.com

For Ian, who left us all too soon.

Chapter One

Lorcan McFadden sat at a small, round, and badly stained table in the pub he called his local. The pub was largely empty with just one or two regulars seated at the bar. It smelled of stale beer, and the carpet was slick with years of spillage and God knows what else its patrons had brought in on their shoes. But it suited Lorcan and his girl well enough, and the drink was cheap.

Lorcan was a tall, skinny lad, with dark shoulder-length hair that fell onto the greasy collar of his anorak. He had a bony, angular face with narrow set eyes that gave him the appearance of a rat. His torn jeans added to the general impression of lack of care, although it was to some extent offset by the brand new expensive white trainers that adorned his otherwise bare feet.

Lorcan was nursing the dregs of a pint of Smithwicks, his second of the evening. It would be his last drink of the day, for Lorcan was stony broke.

Sheila, who had gone to the ladies, re-joined him and drained her own pint glass. The two were not exactly an item, but they spent a good deal of time together, and helped each other to earn a living from petty theft and occasional begging around the tourist spots in Galway city. It was the height of the summer, and the town was full of gullible tourists. Sheila was a pretty girl. Her high cheek bones and steely blue eyes coupled with her long fair hair gave her an aristocratic look that belied her modest background. Her size eight figure fitted neatly into her dark grey roll-neck pullover and blue denim jeans, which unlike Lorcan's, were well kept.

Sheila had left home a year ago when her mother re-married after four years of being a widow. Her mother's new man took more than a shine to his new step-daughter and had made it his business to catch her semi-naked in the bathroom or enter her room at inopportune times to bid her goodnight. She was smart enough to realize that this wasn't going to end well, so she left home at seventeen and made her own way, such as it was, in the seedy margins with Galway's other homeless people.

Her appearance was helpful to her endeavours as a beggar, and she usually managed to clock sixty or seventy euro in a day, while Lorcan kept watch for the ever-present Gardaí who would move them on, or worse still, if the Garda in question was having a bad day, book them for vagrancy.

They were about to leave the bar when a man that they had just recently met, and who had fenced some of their stolen gear, approached and sat down in between them on one of the empty stools.

"All right, Lorcan, Sheila?"

"Yeah, we're good. Just about to leave actually," Lorcan replied.

"Ah, bide a while won't ye? Here, I'll buy you a drink." The man handed a twenty euro note to Sheila who wasted no time in heading to the bar with their empty glasses.

"Well, Lorcan, you drive a car if I remember rightly, don't you?"

"Of course I do, but I haven't any wheels just now. I'm a bit broke," Lorcan replied.

"Right. Well I wonder if you and the girl might be interested in a little job I have out west in the next few days?" the man enquired. "I can fix you up with a car for the job – nothing fancy mind – but it will do."

"Sure, as long as there's a few bob in it," Lorcan replied, trying not to show his eagerness too much. "I'll be glad to be mobile again too."

"Good man, well here's the gig."

Chapter Two

Senior Inspector Mick Hays was sitting at his desk in Mill Street Garda Station when his partner, Inspector Maureen Lyons came in with two mugs of hot coffee.

"What have you got there, Mick?" she said.

"These damn things have started to turn up again," he said, holding up a twenty euro note.

"And they're bloody good ones too. I thought we'd finished with this nonsense last year when we raided that house out on the Limerick road and found the printing press. But these are much higher quality. It wouldn't have been detected at all except for the banknote counting machine that spat it out."

"Where did they come from?" Lyons said.

"Oh, the usual. These two came from different pubs in the city when the landlord was doing the lodgement after the weekend, and I'm sure we're not finished with them yet. I've put out a notification to all the pubs and restaurants to be sure to use their pens on all twenties, but you know yourself, when they are busy they don't bother.

Will you take Eamon out to the bars that these came from and see if there's any CCTV, or if the barmen remember anything about who might have passed them?" Hays said.

"Yes sure, no problem. I never need much encouragement to go calling on pubs, as you know!" Lyons said.

* * *

The first one they called on was The Ostán, which was the Irish name for an inn and was reasonably easy to pronounce for the many visitors that frequented the place every day. It was right in the middle of Galway and enjoyed a vigorous trade. Like many of the pubs in the city it had been given a makeover at the end of the noughties and was now festooned with old books and kitchenalia dotted around on high shelves, with a good smattering of brass running the length of the long mahogany bar. Subdued lighting finished off the atmospherics in the place, and even at 11:30 in the morning, there were quite a few patrons enjoying the somewhat twee hospitality.

The two detectives approached the bar and introduced themselves discreetly, so as not to frighten the locals. After a brief discussion with the owner, a ruddy faced overweight man with thinning grey hair and an enormous beer belly, it was decided that there was no evidence to be collected about who might have exchanged the forged currency for drink at some stage over the previous weekend.

"I wouldn't have said a word about it, only the bank made a fuss. It's an occupational hazard in this job, although we haven't seen much of it for the last few years to be honest," the man said.

"That's 'cos we're doing such a good job keeping it off the streets, sir," Lyons said, tongue in cheek.

"Well you need to do a slightly better job just now, don't you? I can't afford many more of these things in my tills – it's hard enough to make ends meet as it is," he complained.

After a short discussion about crime prevention, and how the bar staff should be using the counterfeit detection pens on all twenties and larger denominations of notes, Lyons and Flynn left and went to the second hostelry on their itinerary.

Things went much the same there, although the manager was a good deal more helpful. This pub did have CCTV, but the cameras were trained on the tills, so that the proprietor could keep an eye on the bar staff, making sure that they rang up every drink sold and weren't on the fiddle. He explained that the pub had enjoyed a really busy weekend, and that it would be totally impossible to tell how the dud note got into the tills.

"It's odd," Lyons said to Flynn on the way back to the station. "If I was washing a dose of iffy notes, I'd buy each drink with a new one, to maximize the return of clean money, but this guy just seems to have been paying for his drink with them and leaving it at that. Very strange."

* * *

It was just coming up to 6:30 pm and Hays and Lyons were getting ready to go home when the phone rang on Hays' desk.

"This is Diarmuid at The Ostán, Inspector, I've just taken one of those forged twenties from a punter. He's still here sipping a pint of beer in the lounge. Thought you might like to know," he said.

"Thanks, yes of course, thanks very much. If he tries to leave before we get there, try to stall him. Offer him a free pint if you have to, but don't let him get away!" Hays said.

Hays and Lyons decided to walk across town to The Ostán, given the time of night, as the traffic would be cruel, and they didn't want to alert their suspect by using sirens. But as they walked along, Hays used his mobile phone to arrange for an unmarked Garda car to pull up outside the pub as soon as possible. It took them just eight minutes to make the journey, and by the time they got there, the unmarked Hyundai was parked outside on the double yellow lines.

Inside the pub, Hays asked for Diarmuid, who was one of three servers behind the bar. Diarmuid pointed out the customer who was alleged to have passed the dud note, and Hays and Lyons went over to him and sat beside him, one either side of the man.

"My name is Senior Inspector Mick Hays, and this is my colleague Inspector Maureen Lyons, sir," Hays said in a quiet voice. "We'd like you to come nice and quietly with us to the Garda station for a wee chat. Please don't make a scene, for your own sake."

The customer feigned bewilderment, but seeing the cold stare in Hays' eyes, decided to comply. They all went outside peacefully where the squad car was waiting to take them back to Mill Street.

* * *

In the interview room, the two detectives established that the man they were talking to was Eddie Turner, an English tourist over in the west for a few days to enjoy the scenery and the craic.

Eddie couldn't explain how it was that he had come to pass a dodgy twenty euro note across the bar at The Ostán.

"I must have been given it in my change he said. I'm not used to this Euro dosh, so I ain't got a clue mate," he protested.

Eddie kept up his story that he must have been given the forged currency in his change, or perhaps at the bureau in Dublin Airport. They questioned him for a further half hour, telling him that it was a serious matter passing forged currency, but could get no further with the story, so they decided to leave him for a while to think on his plight, while they went and made some further enquiries.

Fortunately, Sinéad Loughran was still working in the forensic lab attached to the station, and when Lyons called her, she was happy to come across to see if there were any forensic details on the notes that could link them to the man helping with enquiries. In the meantime, Hays had sent Detective Sergeant Eamon Flynn off to Eddie Turner's hotel room to give it the once over and see if the man had a stash of more notes hidden away anywhere.

"It's hopeless, sir. The notes have been handled a lot, and there's nothing but smudges all over them. I'm sorry, but I'm not going to get any decent prints off any of this lot. Anyway, even if I could get a set of prints, that doesn't prove that the man's story isn't true. I'm really sorry," Sinéad said.

"OK, Sinéad, thanks for trying anyway. Can you take them away and see if you can find out anything more about them for us? You know, where the paper was made, anything relevant about the ink that was used – all the usual," Hays said.

"Yes, of course, sir," Sinéad said, picking up the notes and tucking them neatly into a plastic evidence bag.

"What do you reckon, boss?" Lyons said after the forensics girl had left.

"I don't know Maureen. Give Eamon a call and see if he has come up with anything at the hotel. If not, we'll have to let him go. Maybe we've put the wind up him enough to stop his little game anyway," Hays said.

A few minutes later, Lyons was back in Hays' office.

"Eamon got nothing, boss. The room is clean – well sort of. It's not a very upmarket hotel, but Eddie just has a few clothes, toiletries, a map of County Galway and a copy of last week's Daily Mirror, oh and a betting slip. You guessed it – €20 to win on a horse at Redcar with Paddy Power – but it didn't," she said.

"Didn't what?"

"Didn't win."

"Oh right, so strictly speaking Paddy Power are not at any actual loss if Eddie used one of his homemade notes, so we needn't worry about that then," Hays said.

They had another interview with Eddie telling him that it was a serious matter, and they needed to know where he had got the forgeries, but he stuck rigidly to his story, and eventually they decided to release him for lack of evidence. They told him they were keeping his forged notes though, much to his disgust.

"I paid good sterling money for those, I'm out of pocket now," he protested, but the Gardaí were having none of it and he was sent packing a poorer but a wiser man.

Chapter Three

It was late June in Connemara. It had been one of those unusual summers in the west of Ireland with a seemingly endless string of clear, sunny, warm days, just occasionally punctuated by one rainy day here and there, 'just to remind us it can,' as the locals would say.

The landscape looked truly magnificent in the bright sunshine, and the strong yellow gorse set against the backdrop of the blue of the mountains painted an unbelievably beautiful vista.

Tourists thronged the area in their hired cars and on bicycles, filling the hotels and hundreds of guest houses all along the Wild Atlantic Way. It was going to be a bumper season this year for sure.

Bernard Craigue, his wife Hannah and their twenty-year-old son, Jeremy, had spent an enjoyable day touring around the area in the comfort of Bernard's navy-blue Jaguar. They had left their substantial bungalow overlooking the strand at Ballyconneely soon after 10 a.m. and had driven out across the bog on the narrow undulating roads as far as Kylemore Abbey, starting out via Roundstone, and then turning left across country via Glynsk on the Leenaun road, so that they could enjoy more of the incredible scenery.

Bernard was fascinated by the history of the Abbey which came into being when the Benedictine nuns fled from Ypres in Belgium near the start of the First World War. He marvelled at the relics that the nuns had salvaged from their original home and was in awe of the work that they had completed, fully restoring the magnificent walled garden and grounds, and bringing the Abbey itself back to a serviceable, if not luxurious, state. While Bernard was immersing himself in the history of the place, Hannah spent time in the well-stocked gift shop. She bought several slightly tacky mementos to take back to her sister in London, who, in truth, already had quite enough cheap Chinese-made souvenirs of Connemara.

The Craigues had a good lunch at the café attached to the Abbey, and then made their way slowly back through Letterfrack and Clifden to their house in Ballyconneely.

Bernard had bought the house shortly after selling his printing business in north London for twelve million pounds a few years earlier. He had started working in the printing industry in the 1970s, soon after leaving school. He began as an apprentice, lugging quantities of paper and finished printed goods around, and cleaning down the machines at the end of the various print runs. When he had learnt his trade a few years later, he left the company he was with and set up his own very humble operation, initially working from a lock up garage near his rented home in Hendon. With very low overheads, and a modest loan from his family, he quickly grew the business, mostly by approaching clients of the firm he had left and undercutting their prices. By shaving significant amounts off his customers' printing costs, Bernard's company grew rapidly.

By the time Bernard sold the company, it had moved to an industrial estate behind Brent Cross Shopping Centre and employed forty-two people. The price he achieved reflected the value of the long-term contracts that Bernard had negotiated for the printing and distribution of popular women's interest magazines. It was a lucrative trade. As Bernard himself was often known to say, 'We don't just print magazines, we print money!'

The house that the Craigues owned in Ballyconneely was one of the finest in the area. It had been built before Galway County Council had clamped down hard on the type of construction they would allow in Connemara. As a result, it was bigger and more contemporary than many others in the area. A massive feature window running the full width of the main lounge provided spectacular views out over Ballyconneely strand. As soon as Bernard and Hannah saw the house, they knew they had to have it, and probably paid quite a bit over the odds for it – but no matter, they said, it was unique.

Since buying the property, they spent two periods every year holidaying in their new home from home. The month of June, and the last three weeks of September were their favourite times, and Bernard would occasionally come over earlier in the year for a week on his own to check up on things and see to any small maintenance issues.

Jeremy, although being just twenty years old and hence having quite different interests to those of his parents, was happy to accompany them for the June vacation. He was doing Business Studies at London University, and once the end of year exams were over, he was glad to escape to the peace and tranquillity of the west of Ireland to relax and recharge his batteries.

Jeremy was a sociable chap. On most evenings he would ask his father to drive him into Clifden where he would meet up with other young folks on holiday in the area for a few pints and "the craic". Clifden in high summer was jumping, with several of the many bars hosting live traditional music, and Jeremy usually made his way to King's Bar at the top of the town where he was by this time quite well known. He enjoyed chatting to his new friends and they frequently made arrangements to meet the following day for a swim, or to take a boat out to one of the many small islands just off the coast.

Jeremy's habit was to finish up in Clifden soon after ten o'clock, so he could walk back to Ballyconneely in the dusk. The walk was very enjoyable, especially once he got past the narrow road leading out of the town into more open countryside. It usually took him about an hour and a half to complete, and by the time he reached home the cool night air and the exercise ensured that he was stone cold sober, which pleased his mother greatly.

The evening in question was much like any other. Jeremy left King's just after ten, and walked down the main street of Clifden, out across the narrow bridge and on out towards the secondary school. He turned the corner by the smoked salmon factory, strolled across the second bridge and headed for home. Walking along the road, feeling mellow from the beer he had consumed in Clifden, and inspired by the beauty of the surroundings in which he found himself, Jeremy counted his blessings silently to himself. His parents had always looked after him well. He had been sent to a good private school in London when his father was struggling with a new business and didn't have money to spare, and he knew that his parents had foregone holidays and other luxuries to ensure that he got the very best possible start in life. He was a fortunate young man.

The late evening twilight had softened the breeze to a veritable cat's paw and the scent from the hedgerows helped to create an idyllic scene as Jeremy walked along. There was very little traffic on the road, with most of the tourists checked into their hotels and guesthouses by this hour, so there remained just the occasional local making their way towards the town to grab a pint or two before closing after a hard day digging peat or working on the land.

Jeremy was about half way home when he rounded a bend in the road to see an old silver Toyota stopped untidily with its bonnet raised. Standing beside the car, looking helpless in the fading light, was a small, thin, but not unattractive girl with a ponytail, wearing jeans and a zipped up pink jacket and trainers.

"Hello there," said Jeremy, "got car trouble?"

"Oh hi, yes, it just stopped. I don't know what's wrong. There's plenty of fuel," the girl said in a plaintive voice, standing beside the front wing with one hip dropped in a rather provocative pose. "Do you know anything about cars?" she continued.

Jeremy was struck by Sheila's appearance. She was gorgeous, and he thought that if he could get her car going, he could almost certainly cadge a lift from her back to Ballyconneely, and if he used his charm to good effect, who knows what might develop.

"Not much to be honest. But I'll have a look if you like."

"Oh, would you please? I have to get back to Galway tonight. Thanks," she said, smiling warmly at the lad, and turning to show off the best attributes of her neat figure for him to admire.

Jeremy made his way to the front of the car and stuck his head under the bonnet. He fiddled with the wires going into the spark plugs, and pushed a few things around, not really knowing what he was doing, but anxious nevertheless not to appear too clueless in front of the pretty girl.

As he was lifting his head out of the engine bay, saying, "Try it now," a thick wooden baton smashed into the back of his head, and he fell to the ground clumsily, out cold.

"Quick. Help me get him in the boot," Lorcan instructed, as he closed the bonnet of the old car with a loud thud.

"Here," he said, handing the girl a roll of silver duct tape, "tape his mouth and bind his feet with this, and hurry up."

The girl did as she was told. Then the two assailants dragged Jeremy round to the back of the car and bundled him into the boot. Lorcan hopped into the driver's seat, his accomplice beside him, started the car and took off at speed towards Roundstone. Lorcan was well pleased with himself. The whole thing had only taken a minute or two, and there was no one around to see what had taken place.

The plan was to drive to a cottage out at Carna that the man had rented for a week. It was well out of the way and had been stocked with some basic provisions. Lorcan and Sheila were to keep Jeremy at the house while the man made the ransom call to the Craigues. Then, Lorcan would pick up the cash the following evening, bring it back to the cottage, hand over the money to the man, receive his payment of a thousand euro, and leave. Once they were back in Galway, they would phone the Craigues from a public phone and tell them where to pick up their son. Simple.

Chapter Four

Lorcan was not used to driving on narrow, boggy roads, and the suspension of the old car was not the best in any case. With nervous energy still coursing through him from the snatch, he was going too fast and was having a hard time keeping the vehicle under control. As he tried to navigate the S bends at the turn down to Dog's Bay, about a mile before Roundstone village, Lorcan finally lost command of the car. The old Toyota gave up its tenuous grip on the road. It spun around, hitting the bank on the sea side of the road, then flipped over and skidded along on its roof, before coming to rest in a cloud of smoke and steam at the side of the ditch.

Lorcan blacked out for a minute or two as he was thrown around inside the tumbling car. When he came around, his head hurt like hell, and he was bleeding from a cut over his eye. He was upside down, held in by his seat belt. The car was still emitting steam and smoke from the engine bay, and Lorcan's thoughts turned immediately to freeing himself from the wreck in case it caught fire. He found the seat belt button and released it, causing him to fall forward onto the roof of the inverted car, jammed between the shattered windscreen and the seat. He managed to kick the remains of the broken front window out and, scrambling for grip while trying not to cut himself further on the many sharp edges all around him, he stumbled out onto the road.

Dizzy, with his head hurting badly and with his face covered in blood, his thoughts turned to Sheila. He got around to the passenger's side of the car and managed to pull the door open with much renting and scraping. Sheila had not fared as well as Lorcan in the crash. She was unconscious, with a nasty wound on the side of her head that was bleeding quite profusely, and her left arm appeared to be twisted at a crazy angle.

"Sheila, Sheila!" he shouted. Then, louder as he nudged her shoulder, "Sheila, can you hear me?" There was no response.

"Shit, shit, shit," Lorcan shouted to no one in particular.

"We have to get out of here," he said to himself. He spent the next five minutes gently lifting and prising the limp form of the girl away from the seat, and the now deflated white airbag away from her face, and finally got her free. Lorcan had to carry the girl but, although she wasn't heavy, he was not feeling too good himself. He needed to distance them from the scene as soon as possible, so he set off along the narrow, tarred lane that leads down to the beautiful beach at Dog's Bay.

After a few minutes, having stopped to rest a couple of times, the two approached the end of the track where the old abandoned camping site stood. Just before the boarded-up entrance, a half-built cottage, set back in the rocky scrubland, looked as if it could provide some rudimentary shelter for them until Lorcan could sort things out.

The cottage had been partly completed but the owner had run out of money before it was finished. It had windows and doors, and a roof, but the inside was totally barren, with no doors and just the basic concrete block walls dividing up the space. Many of the windows had been broken too, and Lorcan, having set Sheila down on a patch of soft reeds and grass, had no difficulty getting inside through the back door.

He went back and collected the girl. Inside the house he found an old mattress where he laid her down gently, being careful of her broken arm.

There were a couple of old kitchen chairs and a crate that had been used as a table in the room with the mattress. On it were three old mugs, still with mouldy dregs of tea in them. The workmen had used the grate to light a fire, presumably to boil water for their tea and the ash of their last effort, along with a few dried-out sods of turf, remained in the hearth.

* * *

The man waited up for the one-word text message that he had arranged for Lorcan to send once they had got Jeremy back to the hideout in Carna. But it didn't arrive.

"Damn it Lorcan," he said to himself. "They must be back there by now. Maybe there's no signal on his phone. Yes, that will be it. I checked my phone out there, but he's probably not on the same network. Sure, it will be fine. What could possibly go wrong?"

The man stretched out on the sofa in his room and pulled the rug over him. He set his phone to wake him at 5 a.m. and drifted off to sleep.

Chapter Five

The early morning sun streamed in through the dirty broken glass at the half-finished house at Dog's Bay. Lorcan woke with a start. He was sore and stiff, but as he shook off the last of his restless sleep, he checked himself over and found that everything seemed to be working.

He knelt beside the still shape of Sheila and nudged her shoulder.

"Sheila, Sheila, wake up. It's morning," he urged.

Sheila's eyes opened slowly, and she looked up at him.

"Where are we?" she murmured, "what happened?"

"We had a car crash. You're quite badly hurt."

"Oh God, don't I know it. My arm hurts like hell, and I'm frozen stiff."

Sheila tried to get up using her good arm as a pivot, but she couldn't make it work, and she collapsed back down onto the mattress with a yelp. Lorcan noticed that the severe gash she had on her head had begun to ooze blood again.

"You've got to go and get help Lorcan. I'm not in good shape. My arm's broken and I'm dizzy and cold. Help me please," she implored.

"OK, OK. I'll go and get some stuff. I'll be back in a while. You just stay there and rest," he said.

Lorcan made his way out of the back of the house and off across the fields towards Gurteen. He gave two obviously occupied houses a wide berth, although at six-thirty in the morning there was no one at all around. The third cottage he came to, overlooking the strand at Gurteen, appeared to be empty. He circled it quietly, noting that none of the curtains were closed, and there were no vehicles outside. He approached the rear of the property and after a final check to see that it really was unoccupied, and there was no one observing him, he smashed the glass in the back door and let himself in.

Lorcan wasted no time in rounding up as much as he could easily carry back to Sheila. He took two large fluffy towels, some paracetamol that he found in the bathroom cabinet, and he filled a litre bottle of water from the kitchen tap and helped himself to two unopened packets of biscuits that had been left in one of the kitchen cabinets.

He was back at the abandoned house with his small consignment of provisions twenty minutes later. Sheila appeared to have gone downhill in his absence. She was drifting in and out of consciousness and wasn't making any sense when she tried to speak. He managed to get a few painkillers into her, but he didn't like the way she was shivering, and she looked so very pale. He would have to get her to a hospital and that meant he needed a car, and quickly.

Lorcan set out again with just one thing on his mind. He needed to steal a car so he could get Sheila to a hospital as soon as possible. He crossed the fields again and walked around by the narrow little coastal road into Roundstone, which was barely more than a track, but it was useful for keeping him off the main road. He was looking for an older car, and hopefully one that wouldn't be missed for a few hours. He emerged back out onto the main road just west of the village, and walked purposefully on, skirting the main street by walking down by the shore, and on down to the harbour. At the harbour he found his target. It was a small white Citroen van that looked serviceable, even though it was more than ten years old. The van had been left unlocked, so it only took Lorcan a few seconds to hot wire it and drive off. He was fairly certain no one had seen him too. The van drove well for an old vehicle, and mercifully was three quarters full of diesel. Lorcan drove to the car park at Gurteen Bay and parked the van pointing back the way he had come in case a quick getaway was needed. He headed back up over the graveyard and across the rocky field to the old cottage to collect Sheila. There was still no activity anywhere around at that early hour of the morning.

Back in the house, he hurried to where he had left Sheila on the dirty mattress.

"Come on Sheila, get up. We've got to go," he called, but there was no reply. He found her lying on her back, her lifeless eyes staring, unseeing, at the ceiling. The skin on her face had gone blue. Sheila was dead.

Chapter Six

Paddy McKeever arrived at the An Post sorting office at 5:30 a.m. as usual. He loaded his little green and white van with the five bags of mail that he would deliver throughout the morning on his route out to Clifden. Paddy had been a postman for almost forty years and enjoyed the peculiar hours and free time that went with the job. For the last four years, since the last restructuring in An Post, his routine had been the same.

He left the depot at around six each weekday morning and drove directly to Moycullen. Here he delivered the post himself to the businesses and houses in the town, and would be on his way again by 6:45. In Oughterard, the routine was different. The town had its own postman, so Paddy left the bag of mail in a locked box in the main street and carried on out west. At Maam Cross, and again at Recess, he delivered anything that was required, turned off the N59 onto the N341 and headed to Roundstone. He always stopped at Lahinch Castle on his way and was usually greeted warmly by the night porter who was finishing his shift at that early hour. The night porter always gave him a cup of tea and a few slices of hot buttered toast, and the two of them nattered on about the guests that were staying in the hotel, and what they had been up to.

By eight o'clock Paddy would arrive in Roundstone and leave any mail for the town in Frawley's shop, or even outside on the step if the shop wasn't open. Here, the post would be collected by the town's people later in the day, and anything that they wanted to send away would be collected by Paddy in the same shop on his return journey. It was all a bit unorthodox, but it worked well, as there was no official post office in Roundstone.

With his business finished in the village, Paddy left Roundstone and drove out along the old bog road towards Ballyconneely. He passed the turn for Gurteen and continued up the gentle rise in the road, admiring the view of the sea and the beaches as he went. As he rounded the bends at the turn down to Dog's Bay, he came across the upturned Toyota.

"Dear God in heaven," he said as he pulled the little van to a halt in front of the wreck. Paddy got out and walked over to the upturned car. He quickly established that there was no one inside but was concerned to see a good lot of dried blood on the deflated airbags, and on what was left of the smashed windscreen which was lying in the road not far from the car.

When he'd had a good look round the stricken vehicle, he dug his old Nokia push button phone out from his inside pocket. He had tried to change to a smart phone at Christmas when his daughter had bought him a present of an iPhone, but he never mastered it, and used the excuse that he couldn't get a signal on it out in the west, which was partly true in any case.

Paddy dialled Pascal Brosnan – the local Roundstone Garda. The station was a one-man operation, located at the edge of the village close to the Catholic church. Roundstone had somehow managed to dodge the swingeing cuts that saw the closure of over a hundred rural Garda stations in 2011, following the financial crisis of a few years earlier. Furthermore, the old and rather down-at-heel station in the main street had been sold off for development, and a smart new, purpose-built station, modest in size, but functional nevertheless, had been provided out beyond the church standing on a large plot.

Garda Brosnan, who lived in a tidy little bungalow a few hundred metres further down the road from the Garda station, opened up every morning at 9 a.m. Out of hours he had the station phone switched through to his house or mobile. He was surprised to be getting a call this early in the morning, but answered it nevertheless on the third ring.

"Garda Brosnan," he announced.

"Pascal, thank God you're there," said the postman making a rather unnecessary observation.

"This is Paddy. I'm on the road out at the Dog's Bay turn. There's a car crashed and upside down in the road," Paddy reported, still not quite believing what he was looking at.

"Good God, Paddy, is there anyone in it?"

"No, no I don't think so, but there's quite a lot of blood around, and on the road, but no sign of anyone. Will you come out?" Paddy said.

"Sure of course I will. I'll see you there right away. Don't touch anything Paddy – wait till I get there," Brosnan instructed, reaching for his jacket from the back of the kitchen chair where he had been sitting eating his breakfast.

* * *

A few minutes later Pascal Brosnan arrived at the scene in his brightly coloured Garda car. He got out of the vehicle and put on his peaked cap as he made his way across to where Paddy was standing beside the wreck.

"God, that's a fine mess you've brought me, Paddy," Brosnan said as he started a preliminary investigation of the upturned car.

"Well, the engine is cold, so it must have happened during the night. I wonder where the occupants have got to?" he said to no one in particular, observing drops of dried blood on the tarmac leading away from the vehicle.

"Looks like there was a driver and a passenger, judging by the blood on the airbags," Brosnan went on, "but we can't leave it here. I'll give Tadgh Deasy a call and get him out to take it away."

Tadgh Deasy ran a garage of sorts a few miles out beyond Roundstone on the Recess road. He dabbled in tractors, trailers, vans and he even bought and sold the occasional second-hand car. He had an uneasy but relatively peaceful relationship with the Gardaí. They were suspicious about the provenance of some of Deasy's stock, but they also relied on him to help out in situations like this, so they didn't examine his operation too closely, unless a complaint was made.

Tadgh Deasy was only just up when he got the call from Pascal Brosnan. He told the Garda he would be along in about half an hour, and he'd be bringing his son Shay to lend a hand.

Garda Brosnan thanked Paddy for his help and sent him on his way, saying that he might be required to come into the Garda station over the next few days to make a statement, depending on what more was discovered. Paddy got back into his van and drove on towards Ballyconneely and then into Clifden where he would spend an hour or two chatting to the locals, and maybe get a spot of early lunch, before reversing his morning route back into the city. He normally got back to Galway around two, having collected any outgoing post at Frawley's in Roundstone, and emptied the post boxes in Oughterard and Moycullen. From two o'clock onwards the day was his own, which suited him well – leaving him free to do a few jobs as a painter and odd-job man which supplemented his modest income from An Post.

Garda Brosnan could hear Deasy's noisy old truck coming from a good way off. Deasy stopped the machine with a squeal of brakes and a cloud of blue smoke and hopped down onto the roadside.

"Jaysus, Pascal, that's a right mess. It wasn't much of a car before, but it's just scrap metal now!"

"Well can you get it outta here for us? You'd better leave it round the back of the station since there were injuries involved. Do you need a hand to load it?" the Garda asked.

"Na, you're grand. Shay here will help me to hook it up."

Tadgh and Shay Deasy busied themselves positioning the truck alongside the upturned car. They extended hydraulic steady bars out to the side of the tow truck and wrapped strong canvas straps around the underside of the old Toyota, before connecting them to a hook on the on-board crane.

Then Tadgh started working the levers at the back of the cab, and with a lot of groaning and creaking, the smashed car slowly released itself from the road and ditch and rose precariously into the air. When the car was dangling alongside and above the load area of the truck, Deasy swung it across until it was positioned directly over the flat back.

The controls Deasy was using to manoeuvre the wreck were greasy and as he went to lower the car onto the load area, his hand slipped on the lever, and the old Toyota fell, still upside down, with a heavy thud, a full three feet onto the back of the old tow truck.

At this point, three things happened at once.

Deasy shouted, "Fuck! Stand clear," hoping that the car wouldn't roll sideways and end up back on the road. The second thing that happened was that the boot of the old Toyota sprang open, dislodged by the sudden bang the car had sustained when Deasy dropped it. Thirdly, Jeremy Craigue's body fell out, firstly onto the very back edge of the old lorry, and then rolling over and falling further onto the road, landing with a sickening slap on the cold tarmac.

"Good Jesus," shouted Brosnan. "Stand back. Christ!" He rushed towards the gagged and bound body of the young man. He felt the side of the boy's neck for a pulse, but the cold clammy feel of the lad's skin told the Garda that life had left this person some time ago.

Chapter Seven

Mick Hays was putting the last of his equipment and provisions into his jeep. He had booked a couple of days off work and was looking forward to spending time on his old Windermere Folkboat that he kept moored at the Galway Sea Sailing Club in Renville.

Hays had a long history with boats. When he was a young lad, his father would drive him out to Carraroe in their old Ford Escort to the little jetty where Hays' uncle Pat kept a Galway hooker. Pat's was a "leath bád" – a "half-boat" – although in truth it was a good bit bigger than half the size of the "bád mór", the full-size vessel. The Galway hooker came in three sizes, none precisely measured, but well known by the locals as the bád mór, the leath bád and the much smaller "pucán". The boats were constructed with a wide beam and a shallow draft, to allow for the tides along the shoreline of Galway Bay where they were often used for prawn fishing or seaweed harvesting. The hookers typically had a black hull, reflecting the pitch that the originals were covered in some hundred years ago, and they were equipped with a single mast and three sails – a massive main sail, and two foresails, all made of rust-coloured canvas. To compensate for the over-canvassing of the boat, ballast was carried in the form of large rocks, some weighting up to 50 pounds, in the bilges. In a heavy sea, when the boat was on a beat, or heeled over, the crew would move the ballast to the high side in order to bring the boat back onto an even keel. Going about had to be timed with some precision, as otherwise the boat could easily capsize if the ballast was piled up on the leeward side, and several of the boats had been lost due to inexperienced handling by less than competent boat men. But if you knew what you were doing, the hooker was a useful and very manageable vessel.

As a young boy, Hays would tie a string of hooks with coloured feathers, and dangle them over the side of the boat, and he often caught as many as fifty or sixty mackerel in an afternoon in July or August when the sea had warmed up enough for the fish to rise to near the surface to feed on minnows and sticklebacks. When they got back to the city in the early evening, Hays would go from door to door near his home, selling the fresh mackerel for a penny a piece, having left an adequate ration with his mother who would gut them, and fry them on a dry pan smeared in mustard for supper.

These early seafaring adventures with his father and his uncle gave the young man both a love of, and a healthy respect for the seas around Galway Bay. If the sea was "up" as his uncle would say, it was Hays' job to operate the little yellow plastic pump to expel the sea water that had sloshed over the side of the hooker when she was being sailed too hard into the wind, but his uncle Pat knew the limitations of the boat and his crew, and never put them in any real danger.

Hays had bought the Folkboat from an older man three years previously. The owner was no longer able to keep up the maintenance on the wooden vessel, nor was he any longer fit enough to sail her comfortably.

Hays had put a lot of work into the boat over the three winters that he had owned it and she was now a splendid example of the class. He had re-done all the rigging, bringing the lanyards and sheets back into the cockpit so he could easily manage the boat on his own, if required. Detective Hays was a tall, muscular and slim man, and kept in shape with as much regular exercise as his job would permit. He was proud of his physique, which was also much admired by Maureen Lyons, his partner. He ate well too, but sparingly, and although he enjoyed a glass or two of red wine with Maureen in the evenings, he was a modest drinker.

Unfortunately, Maureen was hopeless on the boat. She had tried to go sailing with him on several occasions, but it just didn't work out. She got thoroughly seasick, which was no fun for either of them, so when Hays went sailing, she stayed on dry land.

He was just locking up the house when his mobile rang.

"Mick, it's me," Lyons said. "I've had a call from Séan Mulholland. There's something going down out at Dog's Bay. Looks like they have found a body. It's all a bit unclear, but I'm heading out there anyway to see what's going on. I thought you should know."

"Oh, OK, thanks. Do you need me to attend?" he asked.

"No, no, it's fine. I'll take Eamon out with me. I just thought you should know. I'll give you a call when I find out what's happening. Will you be reachable?" she asked.

"Yes, I'll stay close to the shore, there's always a signal there," he said.

"OK, talk soon," she said.

Hays was relieved to find that he could continue with his planned day off on the boat. God knows, it didn't happen very often, so every day snatched away from the toil of fighting crime was to be treasured.

With the fine weather and a calm sea, he would enjoy sailing the boat out into Galway Bay, past the golf resort and on out to Cregcarragh. Maybe he would get as far as Ballymanagh where he could drop anchor and have his lunch.

Hays took the box of basic provisions he had put together earlier on board the Folkboat. He had packed four litres of drinking water, some sandwiches and a few biscuits. The boat had a tiny galley just inside the hatch, with a two-ring gas burner, gimballed, so it could be used when the vessel was heeled over without spilling the contents of the kettle or saucepan.

He cast off from the jetty and motored out into the middle of the inlet before hauling up the mainsail. When he had it set, it filled with the gentle breeze, and he set off in a westerly direction, heading for the open sea of Galway Bay. Once underway, he unfurled the genoa too, so that he could take best advantage of the little wind there was. The Folkboat made a pretty sight, its sails full and gently heeled over, cutting its way through the blue waters of Galway Bay in the sunshine.

* * *

On the drive out to Roundstone, Detective Sergeant Eamon Flynn called ahead to see if they could get any further information from the scene. Flynn had been made up to sergeant soon after Maureen Lyons had successfully completed her inspector's exams. He deserved the promotion, and happily took on the added responsibility. Although he was in his early thirties, he had no steady girlfriend or partner as yet, which was a bit surprising, given that he was an attractive man, and a good prospect for any eligible young woman who sought the security of a husband in the force. He liked Sally Fahy, and he believed that she liked him too, but she already had a boyfriend, and in any case, he thought that one pair of partners on the team was probably as much as the superintendent would tolerate.

He managed to get Pascal Brosnan on his mobile, though the signal wasn't good, and the conversation was stilted as a result. He did however ascertain the basics, and when he relayed the information to Lyons who was driving, she had no hesitation in issuing instructions.

"OK, Eamon. You'd better call the lovely Dr Dodd and get him and a few of his white suits out here pronto. And I'm not happy about the driver and passenger of the car either. Let's wait till we get there and see what we can find."

Dr Julian Dodd was the pathologist who worked for the Western Region Detective Unit, based out of Mill Street in Galway. He himself had a laboratory at the Regional Hospital where he performed post-mortems on any suspicious deaths and generally helped the Gardaí with DNA and blood evidence, as well as some of the less savoury material that they encountered from time to time.

While he had a superior and rather pompous air about him, possibly due to his diminutive stature – he stood a mere five foot six inches tall - he was a damn fine doctor and had helped the team to untangle some very tricky cases over the years. Although they would never admit it to his face, the detectives had more than a healthy respect for the man and his investigative powers.

"Good morning, Sergeant Flynn," the doctor answered, seeing Flynn's name come up on his phone, "and what can I do for you this fine summer morning?"

Flynn, who was well aware of the doctor's acerbic temperament, explained the reason for the call and was surprised not to be met with a tirade of protest from the man.

"Excellent," he said, "you've saved me from a gaggle of spotty youths over at the University. I was due to give a lecture to them this morning. I'll be out in about an hour, and for heaven's sake try and keep all and sundry from touching anything and contaminating the evidence till I get there."

"Will do, Doc. Thanks. See you soon."

* * *

When they arrived at the scene they found Pascal Brosnan chatting to Garda Jim Dolan who had arrived in from Clifden. Dolan had stopped his car across the road with its blue lights flashing so that passing vehicles could be directed around Deasy's tow truck and the prone remains of Jeremy Craigue, now covered with a rug, lying in the road.

"For fuck sake," Lyons said before they got out of the car. She was not at all happy at the casual way the scene was being managed.

The two Gardaí stood up straight as Lyons approached.

"Good morning, Inspector," they said in unison.

"Morning men. What's the story?" she replied.

Pascal Brosnan filled Lyons and Flynn in on how Paddy the postman had found the upturned car and how the body had fallen out on the road when it was being lifted onto the truck.

"Where's the postman now?" she asked.

"We sent him off. He has deliveries to make," Brosnan replied.

"Did you get a statement from him?" Lyons said.

"No, but we can get that later – I know his route. He won't be hard to find," Brosnan replied.

"Do we know who the boy is?" she continued.

"No. I don't think he's local though," Garda Brosnan replied, "I don't recognise him."

Lyons donned a pair of blue vinyl gloves and blue plastic overshoes. She approached the body carefully and felt in the pockets with her fingers, fishing out a brown leather wallet from the back of his jeans. Inside she found some euro notes, forty pounds in sterling and a UK driving license with a photo of the dead man bearing the name Jeremy Craigue.

"Does the name Craigue ring a bell with anyone?" Lyons enquired.

"Oh yes, I know them," piped up Jim Dolan. "They are an English family and they have a house out at Ballyconneely. It's a lovely place right there overlooking the strand on the other side of the road from the beach."

"OK. Thanks Jim. Now gather round everyone, here's the plan."

* * *

Maureen Lyons was still settling into the role of detective inspector. She had been made up the previous year following the successful outcome of a particularly nasty murder of an old man in his cottage out near Clifden. Both Hays and the detective unit's superintendent, Finbarr Plunkett, felt she was ready for the promotion, but Maureen herself wasn't so sure. She relied heavily on Hays and wondered if without his guiding hand she could cut it at the senior rank.

"From the look of things, the boy was being taken against his will in the boot of the car. So that's clearly an abduction, or kidnap. I'm concerned about the driver and passenger too. They're obviously injured, and God knows where they are by now. So, Jim, I want you to drive out the far side of Roundstone and set up a roadblock. It may be too late, but you're looking for two people who may well look a bit bashed up. And we need to stay in touch, so call me on my phone when you get it set up."

"Right so," Dolan said, heading for his car.

"Eamon, can you call into Galway and see if Joe Mason and his dog can come out? The kidnappers may still be holed up around here somewhere, and if so, Brutus will find them. There's too many places for us to cover on our own," Lyons instructed.

Brutus, a beautiful black and sable four-year-old German Shepherd was famous in the force for tracking and being able to find almost anything even from the flimsiest trace. The dog had the added advantage that if he found a suspect, he could put the fear of God into them with just a snarl of his sharp white teeth and a bark or two. Joe and Brutus worked as a team as if they were mentally connected, for anyone observing would swear that each knew what the other was thinking. Between them they had helped in the capture of countless villains around the country, and Brutus had earned the respect and admiration of everyone with whom he had worked.

"Right, boss, what are you going to do?" Flynn asked her.

"I'd better go out and call on the Craigues before they hear the news from someone else. You wait here with Pascal and look after the good doctor when he gets here."

"What about Deasy and the wrecked car?"

"He'll have to wait here till the doctor has given the all clear to move the body. Then ask him to drop the car at the back of the Garda station in Roundstone – preferably the right way up! Forensics can do their thing there," she said.

Chapter Eight

Lorcan shook himself awake. After he had found Sheila dead, all the energy and fight went out of him. He had laid down beside the dead girl, sobbing silently, and fallen into an uneasy sleep. His slumber was punctuated with terrifying dreams and when he awoke, he soon realised that the reality of his position was even worse than the nightmares.

He knew he had to get out of there, and soon. He covered Sheila's face with an old musty sack that he found in the house, left the property by the back door, and headed back across the graveyard to Gurteen where he had left the stolen van. He approached it carefully, but there seemed to be no one taking any notice of him. The few campers in the caravan site were just going about their normal routines, so he got back into the van, started it, and headed out towards Roundstone.

He got clear of the village and hadn't travelled far when he came across Garda Dolan's car, parked sideways across the road. Dolan was standing by the car, and seeing the old van coming, stepped into the road and held up his hand.

Lorcan brought the van to a stop and wound down the window.

"Good morning Garda," McFadden said, trying to hide his nervousness.

"Good morning. May I have your name please?" Dolan said, bending down to look into the van through the driver's window.

"Tommy, Tommy Nevin," Lorcan said, keeping his hand over the ignition switch so that the Garda wouldn't see that there was no key in it.

"Well Tommy, where are you heading this morning?"

"I'm going into work in Galway."

"Oh right, what do you work at then?" Dolan asked.

"I'm a maintenance man in a factory down on the docks. I keep the machines running and run errands, that sort of thing," Lorcan replied.

"Have you got your driving license then?" the Garda asked.

"Eh, no, sorry. It's at home I'm afraid," Lorcan said.

"You know you're supposed to carry it on you now, don't you?" Dolan said.

"I'm sorry officer, I just left in a bit of a hurry this morning. I'm running late to be honest," he replied.

"Right. Well I need to look in the back. Can you open it up for me please?"

Lorcan had a moment of panic. He didn't know if the back doors to the old van were locked, and of course he had no keys. He hopped out and walked to the rear of the van and tried the back-door handle. Thankfully, it yielded, and the door opened to reveal nothing but a few paint tins and some old rags.

"Doing a bit of decorating then Tommy?" Dolan said.

"Oh, yes. I'm just giving my sister a hand to do her place up now the good weather is here," he lied.

"And what did you do to your face? Looks nasty," Dolan asked.

"Oh that," Lorcan said, putting his hand up to the cuts and bruises at the side of his head. "It's nothing really. One of the machines at work. A belt broke and whipped up and caught me. It was careless of me. I should have had the guard on it," Lorcan said.

"Right so. I'll not keep you any longer then. Off with you, but no speeding now and watch for the sheep on the road," Dolan said.

Lorcan couldn't believe his luck. He tried not to look too relieved as he got back into the driver's seat of the van. The engine was still running, and he drove slowly around Dolan's car and off down the road. After such a close call, Lorcan decided his best bet was to avoid Galway completely and head for The North of Ireland. He had a good mate in Belfast and he could lie low there for a few days and then maybe get the boat to England.

Before he got to the city, Lorcan turned left, and using the small roads that skirted the base of Lough Corrib, he navigated his way to the N84, and across to the N63 and away towards the north.

The border between the Irish Republic and The North of Ireland is virtually non-existent these days. Since the Good Friday Agreement came into force, all of the border posts that had marked the change in jurisdiction were dismantled, and now the only way you could tell that you had crossed into the United Kingdom was when the speed limit signs changed from kilometres per hour to miles per hour, and the road surface improved measurably. But even so, Lorcan didn't want to take any chances. He would need to swap vehicles before he crossed over in case he met a patrol. He was fairly certain the cop at the roadblock had noted the registration of the van, and it wouldn't be long before they realised it was stolen, so he needed to get rid of it and find a replacement.

Chapter Nine

Maureen Lyons drove out along the old bog road towards Ballyconneely. She was always taken with the sheer beauty of the area, and in the morning sun it looked as good as ever.

She wasn't relishing the task ahead. She had often had to tell parents that their offspring were deceased, usually following a road accident, or sometimes resulting from a drug overdose, but it was never easy. Recently, an increasing number of single vehicle car crashes that often happened in the dead of night, were also suicides. The Gardaí were often able to identify such cases, as there were normally no skid marks on the road, indicating that the car had been driven at speed into the obstacle that subsequently took the young person's life – almost invariably a young man in his late teens or early twenties. Somehow these notifications usually fell to the women in the force, the perception being that they could handle the delicacy of the matter more sympathetically. But try as she would to park her own emotions at these times, Lyons still struggled hard to remain professionally detached.

"I'm just a big softy at heart," she said to herself.

She found the Craigue's house easily and she pulled her car up onto the steep driveway in front of the bungalow. It was as spectacular as she had been led to believe. It sported fresh white paint and sparklingly clean windows, which were not easy to maintain in that condition with the frequent westerly winds that blew in from the Atlantic carrying salt laden spray.

The door was opened by Bernard Craigue.

"Good morning, sir," Lyons said, "are you Mr Craigue?"

"Yes. Who are you?" he responded rather curtly.

Craigue was a short man, no more than 5'7" by Maureen's calculations. He was largely bald, with just a smattering of dark brown hair at the sides of his head that looked suspiciously like it had been dyed. He had a pair of horn-rimmed glasses with thick lenses, and was overweight, with a belly that protruded sufficiently to stretch the fabric at the front of his dark green polo shirt taut.

Lyons held up her Garda warrant card in front of the man's face and at the same time introduced herself. Before she could ask if she could go into the house, Bernard Craigue snapped back.

"What the hell are you doing here?"

Lyons was taken aback by the man's attitude. OK, so he's English she thought, and London at that, but this was not at all what she was expecting.

"I wonder if I might come in for a moment, Mr Craigue?" she asked.

"Well, it's not very convenient just now, but if you must," he said, standing aside to let her in. Bernard Craigue directed Lyons into the lounge with an amazing view out across Ballyconneely strand, looking magnificent in the morning sunlight.

"What's all this about?" Craigue asked when they were seated.

"It's about your son, Jeremy," she said, watching his face and eyes carefully for some indication of what the man might be thinking.

"May I ask where he is right now, sir?" she continued.

"Of course. He's in bed asleep down the corridor. He was out rather late last night, and he often lies in when we're on holiday," Craigue said.

"I see," Lyons said, reaching into her pocket and fetching the driver's license she had recovered at the scene of the car crash.

"Is this Jeremy's?" she asked, offering the man the little plastic card bearing the boy's photograph.

The man took the license and held it between his thumb and forefinger. He was silent for a moment.

"Oh, yes that's Jeremy's. He must have dropped it somewhere."

Bernard Craigue stood up, signalling the discussion was over.

"Thank you very much for bringing it back. He'll be glad to see it," he said.

Lyons stood up too but wasn't quite sure where to direct the conversation next. Did this man really think that his son was asleep down the corridor? It seemed highly unlikely to her. Just as she was about to broach the subject again, a woman came into the room. She had clearly been crying and she was wringing her hands. Before she could say anything, Bernard Craigue started talking again.

"Oh, Hannah. This is Inspector Lyons. They found Jeremy's driving license and the inspector is just returning it. Isn't that kind?" he said, moving towards the door with his hand behind Lyons as if herding her out of the house.

Hannah Craigue was a small, wiry woman with short grey curly hair and a drawn, wrinkled face. The wrinkles extended to her hands, where Lyons noticed her knuckles were enlarged, showing signs of arthritis. She too was short, standing no more than five foot one or two, and although Lyons calculated that she couldn't have been much older than her mid-fifties, a casual observer would have added ten years or even more to that estimate.

"For God's sake, Bernard, tell her!" the woman almost screamed at her husband.

Craigue looked perplexed, as if he wasn't sure what to do next. After a moment filled with tense silence, he said, "You'd better sit down again, Inspector, please," gesturing towards the sofa where Lyons had just been sitting.

"Jeremy isn't here. He didn't come home last night," he said.

"I see," said Lyons.

"And there's more," the man went on, "we got a phone call at five o'clock this morning. Some guy telling us they were holding Jeremy, and if we wanted to see him alive again we are to get a hundred thousand euro together in used notes and await further instructions. They said not to contact the police or Jeremy would be killed."

"Have you heard any more from this person since?" Lyons asked.

"No. But I'm sure he will be back with instructions about the ransom," Craigue said.

"Did he call the house phone, or your mobile?"

"House phone. We leave it connected all year round for the burglar alarm," Craigue explained.

Lyons paused a moment before going on.

"Mr and Mrs Craigue, earlier this morning I was called out to attend a road traffic accident near Roundstone." She went on to explain how the body of a young man had been found at the scene, and that she herself had recovered the license from his wallet.

Hannah Craigue let out a chilling wail and buried her face in her husband's shoulder. She started thumping his chest with her puny fists, shouting, "No, no, dear God, no."

Lyons did her best to comfort the Craigues. They had no relatives nearby, and with the kidnap still in train, there was a need for secrecy, so neighbours could not be called upon. Lyons found a bottle of whiskey in the kitchen and made them both a coffee, generously laced with a good measure of the liquor.

As soon as the couple were settled with their drinks, Lyons went out to the front of the house and called Mick Hays. She outlined the situation to him. When he had digested the new information, he asked, "Do you need me on it, Maureen?"

"Yes, I do, Mick. We still might be able to knobble the kidnapper. It sounds as if there are a few people involved, and some of them may not know that their hostage is dead."

"OK. It will take me a few hours to get out there. But let's get Sally out to the house. We need you back at the station in Roundstone to co-ordinate things. In the meantime, get Flynn out there too in case they ring back. Give me the Craigues landline number, I'll get John O'Connor to see where the early morning call came from. Are you OK?" he asked.

"Yes, I'm fine thanks. Sorry to ruin your day off!"

"Ah what the hell. I'll see you later."

Maureen Lyons summoned the two detectives as Hays had instructed and sat down with the Craigues in an uneasy silence to wait for their arrival. Again, she was feeling unsure of herself. She felt she couldn't manage this situation on her own without calling in her boss. She wasn't happy.

Chapter Ten

Flynn arrived out at the Craigue's house, and Lyons set off back into Roundstone. She stopped at the crash scene to find that Dr Dodd had arrived and was busy examining the body of Jeremy Craigue at the roadside.

Lyons parked her car and wandered over.

"Morning, Doc. Anything for me?" she asked.

"Good morning, Inspector. Well the lad is definitely deceased if that's any help," he said.

"Not really, Doc. Believe it or not, I had managed to work that out all by myself already," she said. "I'm more interested in time and cause of death. Anything?"

"I thought you might be. Time is very difficult, Inspector. It's not like in the movies where we find a conveniently smashed watch face stuck at the time that death occurred. No, this is much harder. You see, it seems he was inside the boot of the car for most of the night, so the usual curve of body temperature cooling will have been distorted. Now if they'd had the decency to leave the boy out in the road, we'd be in business."

Lyons interrupted, "Could you just cut to the chase, Doc?"

"Oh yes, right, sorry. I'd say between 11 p.m. and 2 a.m. approximately, give or take."

"Thanks. And what about the cause of death?"

"Oh, that's simple. The tape around his mouth was partly obstructing his nasal passage, and he'd been drinking quite a bit – beer or lager by the smell. He vomited and choked on it. I'm sure I'll find vomit and a good measure of beer in his lungs when I open him up."

"Lovely. Anything else?" she asked.

"Well, you may get some prints off the duct tape or the bindings on his ankles and wrists. You can't easily apply that stuff while wearing gloves. But I'll leave that to your lot to sort out."

"Right. When will you be doing the PM?" Lyons said.

"0900 tomorrow, Inspector. See you then?" Dodd said.

"Yes, Doc, I'll be there. You know how much I love them!"

The doctor went back to his business, and after a short while the body of Jeremy Craigue was lifted off the road and into the back of an anonymous black Mercedes van that was standing by, before it drove off in the direction of Galway.

Deasy was given the all clear to haul the wrecked car as far as Roundstone Garda station, and told not to handle it if possible so that it would not become contaminated with greasy paw marks.

Just as he pulled away, the small white van containing Joe Mason and Brutus arrived. Lyons walked over and greeted Mason as he climbed out of the van.

"Good morning, Inspector. Lovely bright morning out here isn't it?" he said, full of cheer.

"For some, Joe. Thanks for coming out. How's Brutus?"

"Ready for work, I'd say, after an hour cooped up in the back of this thing. I'll just give him a drink and let him do a wee and then we'll be with you."

"Grand, thanks," Lyons said.

Brutus hopped down out of the back of the van where he had been travelling in a sort of metal cage. He was immediately alert and started sniffing around as soon as he landed on the tarmac. He headed off with Joe for a scamper in the long grass at the side of the road to do his business. When Mason and Brutus came back to where Lyons was standing, she couldn't help but admire the dog. His ears were fully pointed, his eyes bright and his nose wet, and although she really wanted to pet him, she knew better than to confuse the dog.

"OK Joe, here's what we know." Lyons went on to explain the events of the morning.

"We can tell from the blood on the airbags that there were two people in the car, apart from the boy in the boot who died. It looks like the driver and passenger made off after the crash, but I don't think they could have got very far. Can you get Brutus to follow their scent and see if he can find them?"

"No problem. There's enough blood on the road to give Brutus a good start, isn't there boy?" Mason said, stroking the animal's head. Brutus responded by licking his handler's hand and giving a slight bark – more like a grunt really. The two headed off with Brutus pulling on his lead, his snout close to the ground.

"Joe, before you two vanish, can we do a radio check?" Lyons called after him.

"Oh sure, sorry," he replied, and they checked their radios to see that there was a clear signal.

When Mason had gone off with Brutus, Lyons asked Pascal Brosnan to drive out to where Jim Dolan had set up the roadblock and let Dolan leave for an early lunch. She wanted to keep the roadblock in place, at least until Joe Mason and Brutus had finished trying to find the occupants of the car.

Brosnan was just driving through Roundstone when the call came in advising him of the stolen van. He pulled over to take the details from the distraught owner, asking him to make sure that a relative hadn't borrowed it. The owner was adamant that he had left the van where he always did, down by the harbour, and that it had definitely been taken.

"Was the vehicle locked?" Brosnan asked the owner, knowing that the locals in Roundstone rarely secured their vehicles, and often even left the keys in them.

"Not at all, Pascal, not sure who'd be bothered with it," came the reply.

But it was clear to Brosnan that someone had indeed been bothered with it, and more than likely, that someone was connected to the events of earlier.

When Brosnan had all the details, he got on the radio and put out the information on the stolen vehicle. He then continued out to where Jim Dolan was manning the roadblock.

"Hi Jim," Brosnan said as he got out of his own car and sat in the passenger's seat of Dolan's Mondeo. "Anything doing?"

"Jesus, Pascal, I'm in a spot of bother now. You know that stolen van? Well it came through here a couple of hours ago. Looked perfectly normal to me. Just a young fella heading into Galway for work, so I let him go," Dolan said.

"Christ, Jim. You'd better tell Lyons immediately. She'll go ape shit, but it will be worse if you don't tell her."

When Lyons heard the story about how Dolan had let the man slip through his hands she didn't go 'ape shit'. There was no point. She told Garda Dolan to get onto Galway so that they could circulate details of the vehicle, hoping to intercept it before it got to the city. Then she told the two Gardaí to go and get some lunch and go back to the station at Roundstone afterwards. She would meet them there as soon as Mason and Brutus were done.

When they had all gone about their business, Lyons was left on her own at the roadside at the top of the lane leading down to the magnificent white sandy beach. Birds sang in the warm midday sun and the scent of the bright yellow gorse wafted by on the light breeze.

"What a place to die," she said to herself.

* * *

Brutus had no difficulty picking up the scent from the blood on the road surface. Joe Mason had a special lead for the dog that allowed Brutus to go about thirty metres away from his handler but remain under his control. To Brutus, it felt like he was completely free, but Mason could still rein him in if required.

The dog headed down the lane towards the sea, its snout close to the ground, following the trail left by Lorcan and Sheila as they made their escape from the upturned car. About half way down the narrow lane

Brutus stopped, and looked back at Mason as if to say, "C'mon Joe, keep up!"

"All right, I'm coming, take it easy," he said, knowing exactly what the hound was thinking. When Mason caught up with Brutus, the dog set off again, this time leaving the lane, ducking under a wire fence, and taking to the rough, rocky ground to the left of the track. Mason scrambled over a small dry-stone wall so that he could follow.

Brutus was sniffing around among the rushes and stumpy grass, concentrating intently, going this way and that, before he picked up the trail again and moved forward. Soon they arrived at the half-built cottage, and Mason could see that there was a lot of debris and broken glass around. He stopped, called the dog to him and fitted protective leather bootees to Brutus's paws. Brutus knew the drill, and licked Mason's face as if to thank him while Joe was putting his front paws into the little boots.

With his new footwear in place, Brutus approached the house, and soon found the open back door. Mason had him on a short leash now. He wanted them to stay close in case they encountered a hostile situation. It didn't take Brutus long to locate the lifeless body of Sheila lying on the dirty old mattress. The dog lay down on the wet floor and whimpered.

"Good boy, Brutus. Good boy, it's OK," Mason said, patting the dog's head, "there's nothing either of us can do for her now."

Lyons' radio crackled into life.

"Inspector, this is Mason. Do you read?"

"Loud and clear Joe, what's up?"

"You'd better come down here. The old half-built place near the end of the lane on the left. You can get in by the back door, but be careful, there's a lot of broken glass. Over"

"OK. I'm on my way. Out"

Lyons arrived a few minutes later, and entered the dark, damp back room of the little house.

"Jesus," she exclaimed, "this just gets worse and worse." She checked the side of Sheila's neck for a pulse, but the only sensation was that of cold, clammy skin.

"I'll have to call the doc back. I hope he hasn't got too far. And we'll need the forensic team too. Can you see if Brutus here can pick up another scent? The girl wasn't on her own, and the other party may have left some evidence before he got away. Call it in if you find anything," she said.

* * *

"Doctor Dodd, this is Inspector Lyons. I'm still out at Dog's Bay. Where are you?"

"Just having a spot of lunch at Lahinch Castle, Inspector. It's very good. Would you care to join us?" Dodd said.

"Well, sorry to break up the party, Doc, but I need you back out here asap. We've found another body. A girl this time," Lyons replied.

"For heaven's sake, Inspector, this is too much. Perhaps you could make an effort to find them all at once for me," Julian Dodd said.

Lyons ignored the sarcasm. She gave the doctor instructions on where to find the body and went and sat on a rock outside in the sunshine, trying to soak away the chill she was feeling. As she sat there trying to make sense of all that had happened that morning, her mobile phone rang. It was Mick Hays.

"Hi," she said as she answered the phone, "where are you?"

"I've just arrived at the station here in Roundstone. Pascal and Jim are here. Where are you?" he asked.

"I'm outside a deserted cottage on the lane leading down to the beach. Joe Mason is here with Brutus, and they've found the body of a girl. I think she may have been the passenger in the kidnap vehicle."

"Shit. What a mess. Is Dodd there too?"

"He's coming. Fortunately, he'd stopped at Lahinch Castle for lunch on his way back to town. He'll be here in a few minutes. I have Joe, or should I say his dog, sniffing around for any evidence the driver may have left behind," Lyons said.

"Hmm. Pascal and Jim told me about how the driver almost got a police escort away from the scene. Not their finest hour," Hays said.

"I'm going to wait till the doctor has looked over this poor lass, see what she can tell us. Then I'll come back to the station. Can you set up a briefing for, say, three thirty?"

"Yes ma'am. Anything else you'd like me to arrange for you?"

"Well a fortnight in the Caribbean on a luxury liner would be good," she said.

"See you soon," Hays said, hanging up.

Dr Julian Dodd arrived just as Lyons was finishing the call with Hays.

"Well, Inspector, long time no see. How many more cadavers are you going to turn up for me around here today?" the doctor said.

"Let's just get on with it, Doc, shall we? She's in here," Lyons said gesturing towards the house.

Once inside the doctor kneeled down beside the prone form of the dead girl. He examined her head, the degree of stiffness in her limbs, and he took her body temperature.

"She died in the early hours, Inspector, probably around 4 or 5 a.m. Cause of death: loss of blood from the wound you can see plainly at the side of her forehead, coupled with hypothermia. If she'd received medical attention sooner, she would have been fine. But there you go."

"PM tomorrow morning along with the other victim?" Lyons asked.

"Yes indeed. Two for the price of one, as it were," the doctor said.

"So far," she said, giving the doctor a sardonic stare.

Chapter Eleven

Detective Garda Sally Fahy arrived at the Craigue's house in the early afternoon. Jeremy's parents were in an awful state, and Sally set about making strong sugary tea and a light lunch which she insisted that they should at least attempt to eat.

Fahy had been a civilian worker with the Gardaí in Galway up to a year ago. She loved the work, and after a few heart to heart chats with Maureen Lyons, she had been persuaded to sign up. She was clever, and had passed through the basic training in Templemore with distinction. Hays had wasted no time in drafting her into the detective unit, and she had proved her worth. Lyons got on well with her too, although she was aware that as a pretty, smart blonde, she could present some competition for her with Hays. So far, her fears hadn't come to anything.

"When can we see our son?" asked Hannah Craigue, seated at the kitchen table sipping tea.

"Maybe later today. But we need you to stay here for the moment in case the kidnappers call back. They may want to continue with the kidnap, and it's our best chance of catching them," Sally said.

"Surely not. They couldn't be that callous," Bernard Craigue said.

"Depending on how this thing is set up, they may not know everything that has happened, so let's see shall we?" Fahy said.

The two detectives decided that Sally could handle the situation at the house on her own, and that Flynn should go back to Roundstone for the afternoon briefing. The Craigue's house phone had a speaker and a recording feature which would allow her to record any further contact from the kidnappers.

For Fahy and Jeremy's parents the time dragged slowly in the surreal atmosphere. Fahy did her best to engage the Craigues by talking about Jeremy, but they weren't in the mood, so after a few attempts she remained silent.

It was late afternoon when the Craigue's phone suddenly burst into life. Sally let it ring three times before asking Bernard to pick up. She made sure that it was set to 'record'.

"Is that Bernard Craigue?" the man's voice said in a London accent.

"It is."

"Right. Now listen carefully if you want to see your boy again. At exactly eleven thirty tonight, take the money, packed into a supermarket bag, and drive out to the old deserted seaweed factory on the Mannin peninsula. Leave the money on the ground inside the front door and drive off. No funny business. No police if you want to see your boy again," the man said.

Sally nodded to Bernard Craigue.

"Wait, wait," he pleaded into the phone.

"I need to speak to my son. Put him on the line."

The phone went dead.

"Well done, Mr Craigue. That wasn't easy. You were very convincing," Fahy said.

Bernard Craigue buried his head in his hands. Tears flowed from his eyes, and he shook his head silently from side to side.

Sally waited for Hanna Craigue to join her husband on the sofa. Hannah put her arm around his shoulders to try to comfort her husband.

"It's all right, Bernard, it's all right."

Sally called Roundstone and updated the team on what had transpired.

Chapter Twelve

Just after half past three Lyons brought the briefing to order. Hays was happy to let Lyons run the meeting. She stood at the top of the small room where a whiteboard had been set up with photos of the dead faces of Jeremy and the girl, with a red line drawn in coloured marker between the two pictures.

Flynn had arrived back and together with Jim Dolan and Pascal Brosnan they sat attentively, with Hays standing at the back of the room.

"Right folks," Lyons said, tapping her pen on the hard cover of her notebook, "let's see what we've got."

After she had outlined the events of the morning she summarized the position.

"It looks like the girl might have been used to get the boy's attention, and then the driver pops out and gives him a smack on the head, before they both bind and gag him and put him in the boot. Have we got any forensics from the car yet? Prints, whatever," Lyons said.

"They're working on it now. They say they'll probably be able to lift some prints from the steering wheel and maybe the boot lid. The driver wasn't expecting to crash, so he probably didn't think to wipe it clean," Garda Dolan said, anxious to make a positive contribution following his earlier mistake.

"Good, Jim. Follow that up for us as soon as we're done here, will you?" Lyons said.

"So, they have the lad in the car, and presumably they're going to take him somewhere to hold onto him till the ransom is collected. Probably not too far away either," Lyons said.

"That's a real needle in a haystack," said Brosnan, "there are literally hundreds of empty houses around here just now. They might even have rented one."

"Hmmm, you're right. Not much point trying to follow that up unless you get a lead. Any word from Mason?" Lyons said.

"Yes, boss. He called in about ten minutes ago. Brutus followed a trace over to the car park at Gurteen Bay, and then picked it up again. It led down through the village to the harbour, and then went cold," Brosnan said.

"OK, so that will be where he stole the van then, just like the owner said. Thanks, Pascal, you can tell Mason to stand down and be sure to thank him for us. Without him and Brutus we would never have found the girl." Lyons said.

"Right then. Tasks for the rest of the afternoon. Jim, you're going to follow up with forensics on the car. Eamon, will you call Dr Dodd in another half hour or so? See if he can tell us anything about the girl. We need to identify her. Pascal, can you go for a stroll around the village. Chat to the locals, see if you can pick up anything useful, but don't tell them too much. Remember this is an ongoing situation. There may be more to be done out here tonight yet. Let's meet here again at seven for an update," she said, bringing things to a conclusion.

When the team had left to set about their assignments, Hays and Lyons sat down in Pascal Brosnan's office.

"Tea, Mick?"

"Thanks, yes please."

Lyons returned a few minutes later with two mugs of tea and a half-finished packet of chocolate biscuits.

"What do you reckon then?" she asked.

"It's a bit of a mess, Maureen. Two dead bodies, one escaped suspect, and still no clue who's behind it all. Have we done a profile on the Craigues? That might give us something."

"Haven't had a chance, but I'll get John O'Connor working on it back in Galway straight away," she said.

"And ask him to look up any recent kidnappings. I thought all this shit had stopped when the freedom fighters hung up their boots, but maybe not."

"Do you think there could be a subversive connection?" Lyons said.

"It's possible. They are British after all. But we've had none of that crap out here for a good few years now, so I bloody hope not!"

Lyons was uneasy. She sensed that Hays felt that she'd made a mess of things so far, and it didn't sit easy on her. She went back over events in her mind, and apart from the business of Jim Dolan and the roadblock, she couldn't see how she could have done things any differently, and even that wasn't her fault.

Hays was having similar, unspoken thoughts. Had he given her too much responsibility? Was she out of her depth on this one? It was difficult for him as her partner and senior officer to be totally objective. If he'd been out here this morning, would the driver have got away so easily?

"Stop it Mick," he said to himself, "if my aunt had balls she'd be my uncle."

The ringing of the phone on Brosnan's desk broke into his thoughts.

"Hays."

"Oh, hello sir, this is Sally Fahy. I'm out at the Craigues house."

Fahy went on to give details of the phone call that had been received from the man with the ransom instructions. She then played Hays a recording of the phone call.

"OK Sally, that's good work. Why don't you take the Craigues into Galway now to let them identify Jeremy formally for us? Get them to go ahead of you in the Jag in case the place is being watched. You can follow about fifteen minutes behind them and keep a sharp eye out. Then, when you get to the hospital, bring the Craigue's car back out here. We'll need it later on for the drop. Are you OK to lend them yours?"

"Yes, sure boss, that's no problem," she said.

"And get them to stay in the city overnight. The last thing we need is some heroics from a grief-stricken parent getting in the way. Book them into the Imperial and charge it to me."

"Right, boss. See you later then, and will I leave the TV and some lights on in the house?"

"Yes, good idea. Cheers."

Chapter Thirteen

By lunchtime Lorcan McFadden had driven most of the way to the border with Northern Ireland. As he drove along, making sure to stay within the speed limit, he reflected on the events of the previous night and morning. He knew he was in a lot of trouble. Sheila's death had been an awful blow to him. He wasn't that close to her, but still, he was devastated by the way she had died, and he blamed himself for it. They had met at a homeless shelter in Galway a few months earlier and had done some shoplifting together from time to time. Sheila would act as a decoy, creating a fuss about the price of an item in a clothes shop while Lorcan filled his back-pack with four or five garments which they would sell later in a pub for a few euros. That's what had given him the idea of using her to entrap Jeremy Craigue after they had been approached by the man. She had been a very pretty girl and had a great figure too, so they were sure Craigue would stop to help her at the side of the road.

Lorcan was supposed to collect the ransom for the man too. But he figured that Jeremy would have been discovered alive and well in the boot of the car at first light and was probably back with his parents in Ballyconneely by now, telling the story of how he had been duped and knocked out at the side of the road.

"Oh, yes, fella," he thought out loud, "that story will be worth an endless supply of pints in Clifden once your cronies get to hear of it."

With their quarry no longer in captivity, the whole gig had gone pear-shaped in Lorcan's mind, so all he had to do now was try and get himself safely away without getting caught.

Lorcan didn't want to cross into Northern Ireland in the van. He thought that there might be CCTV or even a patrol that by now would have been alerted to the stolen vehicle. He decided to swap the old van, which was running low on fuel in any case, for something a bit smarter.

He pulled into a shopping centre car park on the outskirts of Manorhamilton and parked near the road where he had a good view of everyone coming and going. The centre was a single story, modern building, with a central entrance door, and boasted several of the usual brands for fast food, clothing, and household wares. There was a large supermarket occupying pride of place all along the back of the building. The car park was about half full, with some forty or fifty cars, mostly parked in the marked-out spaces that were inevitably too narrow for the bigger SUVs that had become popular over the recent past. After a few minutes he spotted a woman arriving in a clean looking Ford Focus with Leitrim registration plates. The woman parked the car carefully and got out. She was carrying a shopping bag, and she locked the car and made off into the shopping centre. Lorcan followed her at a discreet distance.

When the woman got inside, she made straight for the café that served the centre on the ground floor and joined another woman of much the same age who was already seated at a small round table.

"Perfect," Lorcan thought, "they'll be chatting for ages and then she'll go shopping. I'll get a good hour out of it before she realises her car is gone."

Back outside, Lorcan had a look round for something he could use to open the car. Over in the corner of the car park, where some rubbish had been discarded, he found an old wire coat hanger.

"Perfect," he said to himself. He used the coat hanger as he had done many times before to spring the lock on the driver's door; he sat inside and hot-wired the car, all within the space of ninety seconds. A minute later and he was back on the road heading for Northern Ireland.

The Focus was good to drive and Lorcan was delighted to see that it was almost full of fuel. Unusually for rural Ireland, it was a petrol model, which made it a bit zippier than the usual diesel cars.

As soon as he was a few miles inside the North, Lorcan figured that he probably needed to change cars again. But he liked the Ford, and it was still three quarters full of petrol, so if he kept it, it would see him right as far as Belfast, and perhaps beyond if needs be. He decided on another plan. He knew that there was quite a big car breakers' yard just outside Enniskillen who weren't too fussy. He had had a few dealings with them in the past and he knew the man that ran the place.

Lorcan turned into the yard and brought the car to a halt abeam a dirty old caravan. The door of the caravan was open, as were the windows, and tattered old curtains blew around in the breeze. A mean looking black Alsatian perked up when he saw the visitor, and started barking like crazy, baring its teeth, and straining on the stout chain that was anchored to the jockey wheel of the caravan. A man in his late fifties, massively overweight and dressed in greasy jeans that had once been blue and a filthy grey T-shirt emerged from the caravan and stood at the door.

"Yo, Séamus," Lorcan said, lowering the window of the stolen car. "Can you shut that bloody dog up. Jesus, it has teeth any shark would be proud of."

Séamus uttered a few stern words in the direction of the dog and it lay down on the wet, greasy gravel and whimpered softly.

"Ah, 'tis yourself Lorcan. What about ye?" Séamus said.

"Is it safe to get out?" Lorcan asked, looking nervously at the dog who still had him fixed with a suspicious stare.

"Aye, you're grand. He won't touch you."

Lorcan got out of the car rather cautiously and stepped well out of reach of the beast.

"I need some Northern Ireland plates on this one Séamus, and a matching tax disc if you have it."

"I'll see what I can do for you, lad, but it will cost you fifty quid, no messing," Séamus said, stepping down from the old caravan.

"Aw, fuck it Séamus, I'm skint. Will twenty euro not do you?"

"Is that all you've got? Aw c'mon, I'll do you a favour just this once, but you'll owe me, OK?"

"Thanks, Séamus, you're a star. I'll bring you something tasty next time I'm in these parts, I promise," Lorcan said.

"Where did you snag this nice little motor then?" Séamus said.

"Ah, you don't want to know Séamus, but it's a tidy one all right."

Séamus disappeared behind a pile of broken cars stacked on top of each other, and emerged a few minutes later carrying a pair of Northern Ireland registration plates.

"These are from a Focus just like yours," he said, "it's even the same colour. And you're in luck, I have the disc too."

Séamus took just a few minutes to swap the plates on the car, and then went back into the caravan, appearing a couple of moments later with the small round tax disc in his grubby hands. He fitted it to the windscreen with a plastic holder, removing the Irish tax and insurance discs so that the car would look authentic.

Lorcan drove back out of the yard. The Focus had been transformed into a Northern Ireland car of the same make and colour and had the matching tax disc on display in the windscreen. For the first time since the accident, Lorcan began to relax. When I get to Belfast, he mused, I might just take the ferry to Scotland and get away from the horror of the last twenty-four hours. He doubted that the man would be looking for him, he would have enough to worry about – not getting the ransom and all.

Chapter Fourteen

Hays was still sitting at Pascal Brosnan's desk, deep in thought, when Sinéad – the pretty blonde forensic team leader – appeared in the doorway. She was dressed in a white scene-of-crime suit, with blue plastic gloves and overshoes.

"Penny for them, sir?" she said, knocking gently on the office door.

"Oh, sorry Sinéad, I was miles away. Come in. What have you got?" Hays said.

"Fingerprints," Sinéad said.

"Fingerprints?"

"Yes, from the car. Steering wheel, B posts, boot lid, door frames – in fact all over."

"OK. Good. Now all we need to know is whom they belong to," Hays said.

"Already done, sir. We have this new kit that allows me to transmit the prints back to Galway where they can look it up on the database. John O'Connor found a match almost immediately," Sinéad said.

"Clev-er. So?"

"So. The driver is one Lorcan McFadden. Small time criminal. He's done a few short stretches for car theft. Nothing heavy. Nothing like this," Sinéad said.

"That figures. And the girl?"

"Sheila. Sheila O'Rourke. Even smaller time petty thief. Done a few times for shoplifting, but never been inside. Got off with cautions mostly," Sinéad said.

"Doesn't sound like either of these master criminals set this lot up, does it? I don't suppose your new-fangled gadget can tell us where McFadden is now?"

"No sir, although I think we're getting that one next month!" she said, smiling.

"What about the car?" Hays said.

"Well I don't think it's going to pass its NCT test this year I'm afraid. But here's the odd thing. It's not stolen, but it's not legit either. It's been through lots of pairs of hands recently, but not nicked."

"OK. Well, see what else you can find out, if anything. And make sure we capture the DNA samples and all that other funky stuff you're so fond of," Hays said.

"Yes sir, of course," Sinéad said.

She was about to leave the office when she turned and said to Hays, "Is everything all right, sir?"

"Well, Sinéad, two dead bodies and an escaped kidnapper. A demand for a hundred thousand euro in used notes, and a sting to set up. What do you think?"

"Sorry sir, it's just …"

"Yes, I know, I'm not my usual bouncy self. It's just that in two minutes I have to phone Superintendent Plunkett and give him the good news. I'm really looking forward to that one. Anyway, don't mind me. I'll be fine. If you see Inspector Lyons outside there, ask her to come in, will you? Oh, and Sinéad, thanks, that's good work."

Lyons returned to the office just as Hays was finishing his call with the superintendent.

"Yes sir. Of course, sir. No, sir, I won't allow that to happen. Yes, sir. Of course, sir. At once, sir."

"Jesus, Mick, he sounds in good form," Lyons said.

"Well you can't really blame him. So far, it's a giant cock up. But I promised him we'd nick the bagman tonight, so let's get started. Can you get the troops back in for six o'clock? And get some food in, I'm starving," he said.

Lyons knew better than to challenge Hays when he was in this humour, but she wasn't happy. It was clear that he felt that if he'd been running the show, things would be working out differently, and a good deal better at that. She felt that was unfair, but this wasn't the time to bring it up. She got on the radios and asked the team to head back to the station, and to bring back some sandwiches, crisps and chocolate biscuits for an improvised meal.

* * *

Hays stood at the front of the group this time. He was still dressed in the casual clothes he had been wearing for the boat. His pale chinos, light blue cable stitch jumper and docksiders made him look several years younger than he usually did at work where he normally wore a sombre suit. Although she was a bit miffed that he had clearly taken charge, Lyons knew why she found him so irresistible. Lyons was both relieved and upset. Things were definitely not going well, but she couldn't see how she was to blame, or indeed how she could have done things any differently. For now though, the important thing was to try to salvage something from the mess and if Hays could manage that somehow, then things would improve for all of them.

"Right, listen up everyone," Hays said, rubbing a few remaining crumbs from the front of his pullover.

"I think it's fair to assume that after the crash last night, the driver and his accomplice took off without too much thought about the original plan, nor indeed the welfare of their victim. I'm guessing they were supposed to take him to a hideout somewhere, and Lorcan was probably going to pick up the ransom tonight."

"That's a bit of a stretch, isn't it, boss?" said Flynn.

"Well maybe it is Eamon. But John O'Connor has confirmed that the call to the Craigues with instructions for the drop came from a pay-as-you-go mobile in West Dublin. So, as I suspected all along, someone other than Lorcan and his girlfriend is behind this, and whoever it is, he was hardly planning to dash across the country when he had a runner here to do his dirty work," Hays said.

"Oh, right. But why is he apparently going ahead trying to collect the money with the kid dead?"

"That's just it," Lyons interjected, "we reckon he doesn't know. We think Lorcan hasn't been in touch. Our man probably thinks that Lorcan and the boy are stashed in the safe house, and that there isn't a signal or something, if he's in Dublin. If that's the case, he has no way of knowing that it's gone pear-shaped – after all, we have at least managed to keep it off the news."

Hays went on. "So, this is the plan. Sally will be back out here with the Craigues car in about half an hour. Eamon, you're going to take it back out to their house and pretend to be Bernard Craigue. You're a good deal taller than Craigue, but if you hunch down in the car, you should be able to fool them, and it'll be dark by the time you set off from the house to the pick-up point in the car, so anyone watching won't know the difference. When you get to the house, fill a supermarket bag with torn up newspaper to look like cash."

"OK, boss. What time do I drop the ransom?"

"He said eleven thirty. So leave at twenty past. Drive to the old seaweed factory and leave the bag inside the main door, and then drive off back towards the house. Stop in one of the little dirt tracks out of sight of the road, but near where the track from Mannin joins the main road in case we need you in a hurry."

"Now, Pascal; Jim. Will you head out to Tadgh Deasy's place now and get him to lend you an old rusty van – a Transit or something. Don't worry about tax or a DOE 'cert, just as long as it's good and beaten up looking, and it goes. Bring it back here as soon as you can," Hays said.

"Righto, boss. We'll be about half an hour," Brosnan said.

"Grand. Off you go then," Hays said.

When the team had dispersed in their various directions, Lyons asked Hays, "So what's the plan?"

"We're going to arrest the bagman. You and Jim will hide in Deasy's van parked beside one of the old empty cottages near the seaweed factory. We'll position Pascal down at the end of the track, just where it joins the main Clifden road. There's a house there with an overgrown garden where he can conceal himself. When our man turns up, we'll catch him red handed carrying the bag. The others will be backup in case he makes a run for it, and as a final backstop, we'll have Eamon out on the road. Then we should be able to find out what all this is about."

"Sounds OK, Mick. I'd be happier if we could have a bit more backup, maybe a couple of Armed Response Unit guys just in case this turkey has a gun," she said.

"So would I, but Plunkett wouldn't hear of it. He's convinced we're dealing with a bunch of amateurs."

"Let's hope so," Lyons said.

* * *

The man had tried several times to make contact with Lorcan McFadden during the day. He had no luck.

"Damn the little shit," he said to himself. "I suppose he's cuddled up with that little slag of his in the cottage with his phone off. Or maybe there's no signal. I'll just have to go and get the money myself."

He set off from Clondalkin in the west of Dublin at five o'clock in his hired Volkswagen Golf. The rush hour traffic on the Naas Road was heavy, which he didn't mind at all, as it guaranteed his anonymity. He fiddled with the sat nav until he finally got it pointed towards Roundstone, and the device informed him that he would be there at just after nine.

Excellent, he thought, that will give me time to stop for some food and do a recce on the drop site before it gets fully dark.

The man's plan was to lift the cash, then drive back to Dublin airport in time for the first flight out to London at seven o'clock the following morning. He would hand over the cash in London later that day. He was supposed to give Lorcan a slice of course, but he could go to hell.

* * *

Garda Pascal Brosnan pulled up beside the freshly painted Garda Station in Roundstone in a battered old Ford Transit. The van wheezed and creaked as he brought it to a halt, and he struggled with the lock on the driver's door to let himself out. The van had once been red, but now the paint was a dull and faded ruddy brown colour, and rust patches had broken out all over the body work. The windscreen had a nasty crack running all the way from corner to corner and there was no sign of a tax disc anywhere to be seen. Brosnan noticed that only one headlight appeared to be working. As he climbed down onto the tarmac, Jim Dolan came over.

"Jesus, Pascal. I hope that old crate will get us as far as Ballyconneely. Is there much fuel in her?" Dolan said.

"Deasy said it's about half full. The gauge isn't working, but I'll take his word for it."

"Well anyway, it's what the boss wanted, so I hope he's happy with it."

The two Gardaí went inside to update Hays on their acquisition.

* * *

The Craigues identified the body of their only son in the morgue at the Regional Hospital, with Sally Fahy and Dr Dodd standing by. Mrs Craigue was completely distraught, and at one stage they thought she would collapse altogether. Bernard Craigue was a bit more composed, but it was very clear that the loss of their only son was something they would never get over. Eventually, when there was no more to be said or done, Sally ushered the two grieving parents away, and took them back into the city where they checked in at the Imperial Hotel on Eyre Square. Sally stayed with them for half an hour or so to see if there was anything further that she could do for them, but they were simply inconsolable, so she left them to it.

Sally Fahy enjoyed the drive back out to Roundstone in Bernard Craigue's big Jaguar. She was a little nervous navigating the narrow twisty streets around the city centre and down by the docks, but once she got onto the open road, she relaxed and began to enjoy the luxury of the big machine greatly. The Jaguar seemed to soak up all the bumps and dips in the road that her own little car felt so much, and at times it was as if she was gliding along on air. The stereo was fantastic, and she tuned in to Galway Bay FM where the afternoon show was filled with relaxing music – just right for the journey she was on after what she had seen in Galway. She had to watch her speed though – the car had a habit of going well over the limit with remarkable ease.

In the late afternoon, the seemingly endless sunshine had given way to patchy cotton wool clouds, and out on the bog beyond Oughterard there was a dappled effect of light and dark on the heathland and the mountains in the distance. There was still quite a bit of traffic about – mostly hire cars with their Europcar or Avis stickers in the rear windows – all travelling at a sedate pace through the scenic landscape. "I could get used to this," Sally thought as the driver of a hired Polo waved her on where the road widened out at Maam Cross. She pressed gently on the accelerator and the big car lunged forward and shot past the little Volkswagen as if it had been released from a cage.

When she got back to the Garda station in Roundstone, Hays was about to start the evening briefing for the operation that lay ahead.

"OK everyone. We leave at nine o'clock. I want us all in position well before the pick-up time. Maureen, you can drive the van. When we get to the road leading down to Mannin we'll let Pascal out, and he can find a comfortable spot, well out of sight, in the garden of the house there. Then we'll drive on down and reverse the van up beside the empty house opposite the factory. I'll go into the old ruin and see if I can find a spot where I can keep an eye on the main entrance without being seen. Maureen and Jim, stay in the van keeping a low profile. As soon as our man has picked up the bag, I'll call you in on the radio and we should be able to nab him easily enough. Just in case he makes a run for it, Pascal can intercept him up at the road, and Eamon won't be too far away if things go really pear-shaped. Any questions?" Hays said.

"Yes, boss. We can assume he'll have a car. What if he manages to get to it somehow and drives off? Deasy's van won't be much use in a pursuit situation," Lyons said to a murmur of laughter around the room.

"Good point, Maureen. Jim, can you get Sergeant Mulholland out to lend a hand. Get him to park up on the Clifden side of the main road but stay out of sight till he hears from us. We don't want to spook the bagman if he's coming out that way from Clifden to collect the money. Tell Mulholland to be prepared to stop our man if he turns back on himself. Tell him not to make any mistake about it this time. Ram his car if necessary – we need to be certain about this. We'll get very little sympathy if this goes wrong, believe me. Oh, and we need to make sure we have good radio contact. We'll do a radio check when everyone is in position. Now you can all relax till nine o'clock," Hays said.

Chapter Fifteen

Lorcan McFadden was quite relaxed as he drove the stolen Ford along the road towards Belfast. He was very tired, not having had much sleep the previous night, and as he came down the steep hill leading into Dungannon the tiredness overcame him and he dozed off for a moment. He came to with a start, and of course the first thing he did was to stand on the brakes, locking up all four wheels, and making control even more difficult. The little car pirouetted around and finally came to rest buried in the side of a Volkswagen van which had been coming the other way. Once again, Lorcan's driving skills had let him down.

Neither driver was hurt, but whatever way Lorcan's car had caught the van, its front wheel on the driver's side had broken off, and the door mirror hung down, suspended by electrical wires. The Focus was bashed all along the left-hand side, and the large plastic front bumper was hanging off one side of the car and resting on the road.

Lorcan got out of the car, as did the other driver who was none too pleased at the encounter.

"For God's sake man, what the hell were you doing?" he shouted in a raised voice. "I've got three more deliveries to make this evening and you've gone and put me off the road."

"I'm sorry mate, I don't know what happened. It just started spinning." Whilst the two continued to exchange pleasantries, they didn't notice a white Vauxhall Astra with two PSNI officers inside on the roundabout at the bottom of the road. Seeing the two vehicles embedded in each other, the police made their way up the hill and stopped at the scene.

The two officers got out of their vehicle. They took one driver apiece and moved them apart so that neither could hear the story the other was telling. After a few minutes of careful note taking, the two officers returned to the front of their patrol car.

Constable Alan McCloskey was first to speak.

"What do you make of it?" he said to the other.

"Just an expensive bit of nonsense. Looks like the Focus lost control coming down the hill. I've seen it here before. The road must be a bit slippery. We better get the tow truck out. They're both going nowhere."

McCloskey walked back over to the Focus and was looking intently at the vehicle.

"Hey, Simon. Come here a minute."

The two officers stood in front of the crumpled Ford.

"There's something not right here," McCloskey said. "The number plate on this car is from 2011, but it's a 2013 model. They changed the rear light cluster and the front grille in 2012, and this is definitely the newer one."

"Hmm, OK. You'd better call it in then, see what's on the computer."

Constable Alan McCloskey used the radio on his coat to call in to the station. He discovered that the plates belonged to a Ford Focus, but that it had been totally wrecked and burnt out a few months previously.

"I think we'd better bring laddy boy in for a while till we sort this out. Can you get a photo of the VIN number off the windscreen on your phone while I talk to the driver?" Wilson said.

"I'm sorry officer, but I really need to keep moving," Lorcan said as the officer approached.

"Any chance of a lift to the station?" he added.

"Oh, I think we can manage that OK. Why don't you sit into the back of the patrol car there? We'll be with you in a minute or two," McCloskey said.

When all three were seated inside the car, McCloskey asked Lorcan where he was headed.

"I'm going to Belfast to meet some mates. Are the trains frequent enough from here?" he asked.

"Oh, aye, they go every half an hour or so." The officer gave his colleague a knowing look.

The patrol car drove around the roundabout and on towards the centre of Dungannon. Lorcan was reassured by the Northern Ireland Railways sign pointing to the station that they passed. He couldn't believe his luck – he was only getting a police escort after all that had happened!

Before they reached the town centre, McCloskey turned the patrol car in between two enormous grey metal gates that must have been thirty feet high. The gates formed part of some serious fortification, presumably left over from the Troubles in the 1970s. There was a tower that overlooked the entire compound and the road outside, and an amount of razor wire, and multiple CCTV cameras were perched on top of the high wall completing the picture of a high security establishment.

"This isn't the train station," Lorcan said, his voice now full of alarm.

"That's right laddie, it's the police station," Wilson said.

"But you said you'd give me a lift to the station!"

"Aye, and we did. We never mentioned the train station though, did we, Alan?"

"No. We just said we'd give you a lift to the station, and here we are," the other officer confirmed.

At the police station, which looked a lot less dismal inside than it did from the outside, McCloskey introduced Lorcan McFadden to the desk sergeant.

"Sergeant, can you find somewhere nice and comfy for our new friend here? We just need to check a few things out, we shouldn't be too long," McCloskey said.

"Sure, I know just the place. Come along with me son, and we'll see if we can find you a cup of tea," the wily old sergeant replied.

Lorcan was ushered down a short, brightly lit corridor and shown into a cell, the strong steel door closing with a distinct thud behind him.

Wilson and McCloskey got to work digging up information on Lorcan's car. Using the VIN number, they were able to establish that it had been allocated to a dealer in Cavan in 2013. They reckoned Lorcan had probably stolen it in the South, and somehow managed to get new plates once he crossed the border. They phoned Cavan Garda Station and told the nature of their enquiry to the young Garda that answered the phone. He said that they needed to talk to the sergeant, and after what seemed like an age, the older man came on the line.

"We have reports of a vehicle matching that description having been stolen from a shopping centre car park in Manorhamilton at around lunchtime. Poor Mrs McGroarty is beside herself it seems. Is the car driveable?" he said.

"I'm afraid Mrs McGroarty is going to have to claim on her insurance, Sergeant. Her car has been involved in an RTA up here in Dungannon, and it's off the road," the PSNI officer said.

"Right so. I'll pass on the good news to the poor woman." The officers in the two jurisdictions exchanged more information about the car, and where it was being taken.

Before hanging up, McCloskey said to the Garda sergeant, "Oh, and while you're there, Sergeant, can you have a look and see if there's anything on a Lorcan McFadden? It was he who was driving Mrs McGroarty's car."

"OK, Constable, but I'll have to call you back. Our system is down at the minute. Will you be there for a while?" said the Garda sergeant, beginning to feel that North-South co-operation was perhaps reaching its limits.

"Yes, sure. We're on till ten tonight. Do you think it will be back by then?"

"Oh, wait, hang on a second. It's just coming back on now. What did you say that name was?"

"McFadden. Lorcan McFadden," the PSNI officer said.

"McFadden, McFadden, eh let's see. Oh, by Jove yes. Seems our colleagues in Galway are anxious to speak to a Lorcan McFadden. Have you got him there?"

"We have. Best if we make him comfortable for the night, I think. We can sort it out tomorrow. Will you let your folks in Galway know we have him safe and secure here in Dungannon?"

* * *

When the sergeant in Cavan had finished his tea, he phoned through to Mill Street Garda station and was put through to John O'Connor. He explained what had transpired, and that Lorcan McFadden was now a guest of Her Majesty in Dungannon police station.

O'Connor wasted no time in calling Hays out in Roundstone to give him the news.

"Good stuff, John. Now can you get back onto Dungannon and ask them to send a photo of the prisoner to you, and then send it on to my phone. I'd like Jim Dolan to confirm the identification before we go creating an international incident," Hays said.

"Sure, will do, boss," O'Connor said and hung up.

Twenty minutes later, Hays' phone pinged, and the photo of McFadden arrived on the screen. Hays showed the mug shot to Jim Dolan, who had no trouble in identifying him as the man who had gone through the roadblock earlier in the day.

"Yes, that's him, the little toe-rag. Of course he gave me a different name, but that's definitely him all the same. What are we going to do now?" Dolan said.

"I'll try and sort something out, Jim. Maureen, can you come with me for a minute?" The two senior officers walked out to Hays' car and got inside.

"OK. This is what we'll do. Will you call Superintendent Plunkett and bring him up to date? He'll be pleased that the driver of the kidnap vehicle is in custody, even if it's in the North. Ask him if he can help us to get McFadden back here without too many formalities. I have a feeling he has connections with someone senior in the PSNI up near the border. He might just be able to swing it," Hays said.

"OK. No problem, but why don't you call him? You're more senior than I am," she said.

"No. It will be better coming from you. Plunkett sees you as a rising star in the force just now, and anyway, this is supposed to be your party. I'm on leave remember. He'll be more inclined to put himself out for you – trust me."

"And you mean to say you're not the blue-eyed boy, Mick?" Lyons said in surprise.

"I thought I was, but I hear otherwise. So, you'll call him, will you?"

"OK. I will. Do you want to listen in?"

"No. You're grand. You can tell me after."

Lyons put the call through to Superintendent Plunkett. He was glad to hear that they had the driver in captivity but wasn't sure if he could do much to help. He did know the Assistant Chief Constable of the PSNI though. They had worked together during the Troubles on some very delicate cases, and although they were from completely different backgrounds, they got along pretty well, and had a healthy respect for each other's professionalism. At the end of the call, he agreed to contact the man and see if he could call in a favour. He told Lyons to keep her phone on, and he'd call her back if he could reach the ACC.

* * *

At fifty-four Finbarr Plunkett had seen most of what life in the Garda Síochana could throw at a person. He had developed strong instincts and a good sense of what would work and what wouldn't when it came to solving crime. His role as Detective Superintendent of the Western Crime Division had changed a lot in the past five years. When he first got the job, you could do more or less whatever was needed to mete out justice, as long as a reasonable result was achieved. But these days with social media in the ascendant and those pesky smart phones with their ever-present cameras, things were very different. Still, Plunkett's sense of fair play persisted, and he was usually able to navigate a safe course between the many, sometimes vicious, criminals that the Gardaí came across and the do-gooders who seemed to be more keen on the criminals' human rights than those of the hapless victims. This meant that he was given a free hand by Garda senior management and he had used this freedom to good effect, building some excellent crime fighting teams that operated out of Galway. Crime statistics in the region were contained, if not reducing, while in other areas of the country the figures seemed to be going relentlessly in the wrong direction. As a result, Plunkett was held in high regard.

* * *

Lyons went back into the Garda station but didn't have to wait long for Plunkett's call.

"Lyons," she answered.

"Ah, Inspector. Yes, I managed to catch the ACC just as he was on his way out to dinner. He made a quick call to Dungannon to see what crimes, if any, McFadden had actually committed in Northern Ireland. It seems the lad hasn't done much there that they can pin on him other than driving carelessly, and they're not too bothered about that. He says you can drive up and collect him tomorrow morning in an unmarked car, with no uniforms on view, and you can have him. But it's important to be discreet. Keep it well below the radar. He's doing us a big favour," Plunkett said.

"Understood, sir, and thank you, that should make things a whole lot simpler for us," Lyons said.

"Glad to help, Inspector. Be sure to keep me updated."

Chapter Sixteen

At a quarter to nine that evening, the full team was assembled in the rather crowded Garda Station in Roundstone. Sally Fahy had arrived back with Bernard Craigue's car, and she confirmed that the Craigues were now in residence at the Imperial Hotel for the night.

Lyons went over the plan once more with everyone before they set out. They sent Eamon Flynn out to the Craigue's house in the Jaguar. He had a supermarket bag stuffed with torn up newspapers beside him, and his instructions were to drive to the old seaweed factory to be there at eleven thirty, drop the bag inside the door, and then drive away, back towards Ballyconneely and stay off the road out of sight, but nearby in case he was needed.

The rest of the team piled into the old rusty Transit donated by Tadgh Deasy. The van was disgusting. It stank of oil and diesel and was strewn with old papers and dirty rags with some dreadful greasy gunge on the floor in the load area. The seats were torn, with dirty orange sponge leaking out between the cracks, and the windscreen was covered in a bluish haze on the inside. Deasy had excelled himself. Lyons drove the van, which wheezed and spluttered through the evening mist across the old bog road, out towards the Mannin peninsula, leaving clouds of pungent blue smoke in their wake. Fortunately, it was still dusk, so the fact that one headlight was out didn't really matter.

They let Pascal Brosnan out as agreed at the junction, and he made off into the overgrown garden of the house at the crossroads and vanished from sight. The rest of the team drove on out to the old seaweed factory.

Lyons had great difficulty engaging reverse gear in the old wreck, but she managed it eventually with much grinding from the ancient gearbox, and with a lot of revving of the tired engine and even more smoke, she reversed the old heap up beside an empty cottage just off the road and nearly opposite their target.

With the van's engine turned off, Lyons checked radio contact with the rest of the team. They had given the stake out the code name 'sea hawk' so that anyone listening in to their conversation would believe it was a fishing boat out off the coast. The van was to be referred to as 'captain' and Brosnan as 'bosun'. It wasn't much of a subterfuge, but it was all they could think of at short notice.

Hays got out of the van by the rear doors and crossed the road to the old building where he found a good vantage point allowing him to see the entrance easily. The building was dirty inside, littered with empty beer cans and old fast food boxes, where the local youth had used it as a shelter for their underage drinks parties. The evening began to turn to night, and the mist got a little thicker, making the old factory look very eerie in the strange half-light, but the Gardaí waited patiently, if a little uneasily for something to happen.

At almost exactly eleven thirty, Eamon Flynn arrived in Craigue's car and stopped outside the old ruin. He got out, and nimbly trotted across to the entrance, clutching the bag of paper in his right hand. He left the bag by the door as instructed and made his way briskly back to the car, and drove off back the way he had come. He avoided looking at the old van parked opposite or making any other gesture that might give their plan away.

A few minutes later, Lyons' radio crackled to life.

"Bosun to captain. A grey VW Golf has just passed the end of the road, turned and come back again this way. Now heading in your direction," Pascal Brosnan said.

"Roger," Lyons said into the radio.

The Golf pulled up on the road just opposite where the van was parked, and its lights went out. The occupant sat in the car for a couple of minutes having a good look round. He then got out of the car. He was a portly man with a round ruddy face, dressed largely in black, with black town shoes and a woolly hat pulled down to just above his eyes.

He made his way cautiously to the front entrance of the old factory, which was now just a rectangular hole in the wall of the building, the door itself having been removed by the elements some time ago. The man found the bag easily and started back towards the road without checking the contents.

"Go!" shouted Lyons, and the two front doors of the old van creaked open. The interior light in the van's cab, which hadn't worked for years, decided at this moment to return to service, and the front windscreen of the van lit up like a lighthouse in the fog.

The man saw the light at once, and a second later he was able to make out the dark shapes of the Gardaí heading in his direction. He took flight immediately. Grasping the bag close to his chest he ran across the rough ground parallel to the road towards the only escape route afforded by the geography of the place.

"Captain to bosun. He's coming in your direction. Single male on foot. Don't let him get away," Lyons wheezed into the radio, out of breath from the sudden chase.

"Roger," came the reassuring reply.

Brosnan, who was used to playing Gaelic games, waited until his quarry was in sight. The man was now clearly running out of breath, but he still progressed quite steadily towards the open road. That is until Brosnan sprang at him from the cover of the hedge and tackled him firmly to the ground.

"Gotcha!" he exclaimed, and Lyons and the rest of them quickly caught up.

"Ah, Eddie we meet again. Small world, eh?" Lyons said.

The man was then handcuffed, still clinging possessively to his bag of old newspaper.

With the pursuit over, Mulholland and Fahy returned with their cars, and everyone but Pascal Brosnan piled in along with the bagman to drive back to Roundstone Garda station. Brosnan was given the unenviable task of returning the van to Deasy with instructions that it was not to be seen on the road again.

Back at the Garda station, Flynn and Fahy were told to take the prisoner back to Galway and put him in the cells for the night.

"What will we charge him with, boss?" Flynn said.

"Nothing", said Lyons, "he's just helping us with our enquiries for now," she said, much to Flynn's surprise.

"Then you get off home, both of you. We'll need you in early tomorrow."

* * *

On the way back to Galway, with the drama out at Roundstone over, for the moment at least, Hays discussed the case with his partner. The two were now living together in his house in Salthill. Lyons had moved in soon after she had been made up to inspector. Although it was an unusual arrangement, the superintendent had said he was willing to turn a blind eye as long as it didn't get in the way of their work. They had made a pact to leave the job at the front door, which sometimes led to a late-night conversation in the front garden, or sitting in one of their cars in the driveway, but they had stuck to it, and so far at least it had served them well. They had discovered that they were physically very compatible on a visit to Poland two years ago when they were working on the Lisa Palowski murder case, and they had grown a lot closer since. Both were strongly independent, with Maureen doing her own hobbies and Mick Hays quite involved with the sailing in his beloved Folkboat. Lyons had even held on to the little flat in the city and sub-let it to a rookie uniformed Garda fresh out of Templemore.

"I'll have it when you get fed up with me and kick me out," she would tease Hays.

"Sure, why would I do that, and you a property mogul," he jibed back at her.

"So, what are your plans?" Hays asked. He was very mindful that it was still her case, despite him being the more senior officer.

"I think I'll head to the wee North in the morning with Eamon to collect McFadden. We'll look pretty inconspicuous driving to Dungannon, just like a couple out for the day. Can you get to work on our latest client and see what you can get out of him other than 'no comment'?"

"That sounds like a plan. Do you think he's the brains behind all this?" Hays said.

"I doubt it. In fact, I think both he and McFadden are pretty thick. That was very amateur tonight – not well thought out at all. He was asking to be lifted if you ask me," Lyons said.

"I'm not sure. If he thought that they still had the boy in captivity, then the bagman would just have been dealing with an irrational parent, not Galway's finest. Their communication has definitely broken down somewhere along the line, that's for sure, but I think McFadden is probably the thick end of the plank. What about the girl?"

"I think we'll leave her to the super-sleuths out in Roundstone and Clifden. It will give them something to do and keep them involved in case anything else blows up."

"OK. But do you think they're up to it?" Hays said.

"Probably. But I don't think she was very important in the grand scheme of things anyway. She probably just went along with McFadden for the adventure and the chance of a few bob. It's a shame about her though, she looked like a nice girl," Lyons said.

"OK. It's your call, and I'm happy to go along with it. I think we may have to step in at some stage if they're getting nowhere. We can't just ignore the death of a young girl out in the bog," Hays said.

"I agree. But we have enough to be doing for now, so let's give them a few days and see what they come up with. When I'm up north tomorrow, why don't you assign Sally as their contact for the case? That way we'll get to know what's happening, and they'll feel that they need to be doing something as well," Lyons said.

"Excellent. Good thinking. I'll tell Mulholland in the morning. That should cheer him up no end," Hays said.

Chapter Seventeen

When the bagman arrived in Galway's Mill Street Garda station, Sergeant Flannery, the night man, processed him as if he was being charged, even though he was officially only helping the Gardaí with their enquiries. He took the man's fingerprints, and relieved him of his bag of cut up newspapers, placing it in an evidence sack, and locking it into the secure store. When the man emptied his pockets, a wallet, mobile phone, driving license, set of car keys and a Ryanair boarding card were all collected. The man was then ushered to a cell, offered some basic catering, and locked up for the night where Flannery would check on him every half hour, and write up the log. During the night, with little else to do, the sergeant examined the contents of the man's wallet, and wrote up the information it revealed on a single sheet of paper, ready to hand to Senior Inspector Hays the following morning.

Hays arrived at the station before eight o'clock. Sergeant Flannery gave him a brief account of the night the man had spent in the cells and handed over the one-page catalogue of the contents of his pockets. Hays studied the sheet with interest.

"Ah yes, Eddie Turner, the twenty euro note man. Forty-seven years old, and from London, no less. Well done, Sergeant. Give me ten minutes and then bring him into the interview room. I'll be down then to start questioning him," Hays said.

Hays spent a few minutes in his office studying the sheet that the sergeant had given him. He then lifted the phone and dialled a UK number. The phone he was calling was answered on the second ring.

"Irene Russell," said the woman's voice on the other end of the line, in an educated British accent.

"Hi Irene. It's Mick Hays here from Galway. How are you keeping?"

"Oh, hi Mick. Haven't heard from you for a while. Yes, all good here. What about with you?"

"Can't complain. Up to my neck in impossible cases as usual. And the do-gooders have us demented. Listen, I was wondering if you could do me a small favour?" Hays said.

"Sure, I didn't think this was a social call. What do you need?" Russell said.

Irene Russell was a Detective Chief Inspector with the Metropolitan Police in London's Scotland Yard. She had been injured in a shooting during a botched bank raid some years previously, and was now desk bound, serving as a senior officer in the Serious Crimes Division of the Met. Hays had met her before she was injured when they were working on a case involving subversives at the tail end of the Troubles in the 1990s, and they had got on well. Using their combined skills, they had managed to lift two very nasty types off a plane at Luton bound for Dublin, and they had assembled enough evidence to put them away for twelve years, although both had since been released under one of the many amnesties that the politicians had arranged since the Troubles officially ended.

"We've lifted a fella by the name of Eddie Turner, or so it says on his driving license. His date of birth is October 3rd, 1970. He's got a London accent, and he came in recently on a flight from there. Just wondering if you have anything on him. I can send over his dabs by email if you like?"

"Ok, well send them on as soon as you can, and I'll have a look for you. What's he done anyway?" Russell said.

"It's messy. He's involved in some way in the kidnapping of a young English guy who was on holidays over here. It all went badly wrong, and the lad died. We lifted Turner trying to collect the ransom last night. Another girl died during the kidnap too, so it's all a bit complicated. And as if that wasn't enough, he also seems to be connected to some dodgy euro currency going around, but I'm not sure of his involvement in that yet."

"Wow, sounds like you have your hands full, Mick. What was the victim's name?"

"Craigue, Jeremy Craigue, son of Bernard and Hannah Craigue. I think they're from Hendon or thereabouts," Hays said.

"Do you want me to have a look at them too, just in case?" Russell said.

"Oh, right. Yes, if you don't mind. Though they seem straight enough, but there might be something. That would be great. Thanks."

Hays and Russell stayed on the phone for a few more minutes chatting about the old days, and how things had changed in policing in recent times, and not for the better, they concluded.

* * *

"Well, Eddie, did you have a good night in the Mill Street Hotel?" Hays asked Eddie Turner when the interview started.

"No comment," Turner replied sullenly.

"Ah now Eddie, you'll have to do better than that I'm afraid. You see we have some pretty serious charges to bring against you here. It would be much better for you if you started talking to us, much better. Now what do you say?"

"No comment."

"Very well. If that's the way you want to play it. But just so you don't get any surprises, here's what we're looking at. Obviously, there's the kidnap. But it's a lot worse than that Eddie. You see, when McFadden and the girl collected their victim, they had a car crash. The lad that was kidnapped died as a result, and then the girl, who was badly injured in the crash, also died. McFadden then absconded and was picked up in the North by the police, on his way to Belfast."

Hays waited for some response from Turner, but none was forthcoming.

"So, you see, Eddie, it seems that you are involved in the death of two people, a kidnap, and a host of other crimes. In fact, the list so far is as long as your arm. So, if you ever want to see daylight again, I suggest you start talking," Hays said.

"I can't. It's more than my life's worth. I ain't saying nothing."

"Well, that's fine, Eddie, just as long as you're happy to take the rap for the whole thing, but by the time we're finished, you're looking at fifteen years. The judges in this country take kidnapping very seriously since the Troubles, and an Englishman in an Irish jail – well, I'll leave you to figure out how well that will go for you," Hays said as he stood and picked his file up from the table, preparing to leave the room.

When he got back to his desk, there was a note to call DCI Irene Russell in London.

He got through almost immediately.

"Hi, Irene. That was quick. What did you find, if anything?" Hays asked.

"Well, your friend Eddie has quite a bit of form. It's mainly burglary, a bit of GBH and aggravated assault, nothing like kidnapping that I can see though," she said.

"Has he done time inside?" Hays asked.

"Yes. He did a six month in The Scrubs a few years ago, and he has a couple of suspended sentences too, and he's wanted for questioning about a few other capers. Is he talking yet?" Russell asked.

"No. Says it's more than his life's worth, but that could all be nonsense. Could I ask you to do a little more digging for us if you have the time?"

"Sure. What do you need?"

"I was wondering if you could have a quick look at his known associates. There's someone bigger than Eddie Turner behind all this stuff, and someone that scares Eddie too, so probably not an amateur. Any information we can get will help us," Hays said.

"Ok. I'll have a dig around, see what I can come up with. I'll try to get back to you later today."

"Thanks very much, Irene, I'll owe you one," Hays said.

"You're dead right there, and don't think I won't collect!" she replied.

* * *

Hays busied himself with writing up the considerable amount of paperwork that the case had generated and updating the Garda PULSE system with everything they knew so far. Then he put a call through to Sergeant Séan Mulholland in Clifden, asking him to get busy with the female passenger that had died in the car crash to see if he could locate her next of kin, who needed to be informed. Mulholland, who was pleased for once to be involved in a genuine criminal case, agreed to take on the task, and said he would inform Hays as soon as he had any information. Hays then briefed Sally Fahy on her role in the matter of the girl, and the Gardaí out in Clifden, and asked her to make sure that progress was being made, and that he was fully informed of any developments.

At twelve o'clock, Superintendent Plunkett phoned him for an update.

"Well, we have the bagman in custody, though he's not saying much, and Lyons has gone North with Eamon Flynn to collect McFadden. So, by evening we should have the two perpetrators safely tucked away," Hays said.

"Hmm, those of them that are left alive at least. Ok, well keep me posted, Mick. Let's get this thing tidied up as soon as possible. We don't want the press getting hold of it. And the boys in Dublin are now calling Galway the murder capital of Ireland, so let's have some good news soon."

Hays had decided to leave Eddie Turner alone for a few hours to stew. He felt that when they got McFadden back, the young man might readily give up a lot more information about the whole thing that would enable them to find out what was really going on.

Hays went out to Doherty's pub for lunch and returned to the station soon after two o'clock. He was sitting at his desk about half an hour later when his phone rang.

Chapter Eighteen

It was almost a four-hour drive to Dungannon from Galway, so Flynn and Lyons left early, just after 7 a.m. It was a bright day, with just the odd brief shower every now and then. Apart from that, it was sunny and clear, and they made good time on the road.

Granard was about half way, so they stopped there soon after nine o'clock at the café in the main street and had a quick breakfast. They reached Dungannon just after eleven, with Lyons who was driving cursing the fact that the speed limits were in miles per hour as soon as they crossed the border, and her car's odometer showed only kilometres per hour. Flynn had translated for her, so that they remained within the law. The last thing they needed was to be pinged by traffic cops for exceeding the speed limit. Their presence would be very awkward to explain.

At the police station in Dungannon, Lorcan McFadden was waiting for them in the main interview room, accompanied by a uniformed PSNI officer. He was handed over without ceremony, and with no paperwork changing hands. He said very little, only grumbling a bit about living in a police state. But he was quite subdued, and they soon had him seated in the rear of Lyons' car, handcuffed, with his hands behind his back. Flynn sat in beside him and made sure that the doors were kiddie locked before they set off so that McFadden couldn't jump out along the way.

The Gardaí didn't feel much like talking to their client, but Flynn was curious about one thing.

"How did you and Sheila meet anyway, Lorcan? She seems to be a bit out of your league," Flynn asked the fugitive.

"Aw shit man, she had to leave home after her ma married that prick Bolger. He's a fucking pedo."

* * *

When they got back across the border, the two detectives relaxed a little. McFadden said he was famished, so they arranged to stop in Cavan, and Lyons went into the Supermac shop and purchased food for the two men. She herself wasn't hungry. After the stop, Flynn transferred to the front passenger's seat, so he could eat his food and give their prisoner a bit of space to do the same. McFadden's handcuffs had been released, and he had been re-cuffed with his hands in front of him so that he could eat his meal.

Lyons set off again as she had no food to eat and was keen to get the rest of the journey completed as soon as possible. Just a few kilometres outside the town, with Flynn still eating, McFadden made his move. He stretched forward and put his cuffed hands over Lyons' head, and then pulled back hard so that he was choking her against the headrest. Flynn dropped his food and released his seatbelt in an effort to get control of the situation, but by now Lyons was choking badly and lost control of the car. The vehicle left the road and careered down an embankment, smashing into a fir tree. Flynn was catapulted forward, and without his seat belt to save him, his head hit the windscreen hard, and he fell in a heap in the passenger footwell, covered in chips and bits of burger.

Lorcan released some of the pressure on Lyons' neck, and instructed her to undo his handcuffs, or he would strangle her there and then. Lyons knew enough to realise that he probably meant it, so reluctantly she reached into her pocket and retrieved the keys, which she then used to release McFadden's handcuffs.

With his hands free, Lorcan elbowed the window in the rear door, shattering it. He then reached out and used the outside handle to open the door. He scrambled out, wrenched open the driver's door and grabbed Lyons roughly by her jacket hauling her out of the car.

"Have you got a gun?" he rasped in her ear.

"Don't be silly, Lorcan. Of course not. We're not armed," she replied.

"Give me your phone," he demanded. "C'mon. Hand it over – now!"

Lyons reached into her jacket pocket and retrieved her phone, handing it to the fugitive.

"Right. We're going back up on the road, and you use your warrant card to stop the first car that comes along. We're taking it," he said.

"What about Eamon? He's badly hurt. We can't just leave him here. He needs medical attention."

"Good enough for him. He'll be fine. Now c'mon, stop wasting time. He dragged her back up the embankment to the road.

"Now, no funny business. Stop the car and then leave it to me, and I strongly suggest you don't try anything funny or you'll regret it."

The first car to appear on the road was a Nissan Almera, driven by an unaccompanied female driver. Lyons held up her hand displaying the warrant card while McFadden stood behind her with her other arm held firmly behind her back.

When the car stopped, McFadden opened the driver's door.

"Out. Now!" he barked at the startled driver. "And give me your phone! Hurry!"

The woman was startled but did what she was told. McFadden pushed Lyons into the car and used his own handcuffs to fasten her wrists together and lock them onto the arm rest. He then got into the driver's seat and restarted the car. As he drove off, Lyons managed to shout to the bewildered woman that there was an injured Garda in a car down in the ditch, and he needed medical help. She hoped the woman would have enough of her wits about her to stop the next car that came along and get help for Flynn, as well as alert the Gardaí to the situation.

McFadden drove the car at alarming speed for about a mile and then turned down a narrow side road which was little more than a track. They bumped along for a short distance, and then he turned into a gateway that led to an old, disused barn. He drove the car partly into the barn and stopped it.

Lyons had not been in this position before, but she had been on courses where this sort of scenario had been played out. She realised however that roleplay on a training course and the real thing were very different.

"What are you going to do, Lorcan?" she asked.

"Watch and learn, Inspector; watch and learn."

McFadden had picked up Lyons' phone and was scrolling through the list of recent calls. He saw that 'Mick' came up quite a bit.

"Who's Mick?" he asked.

"He's my boss. Senior Inspector Mick Hays to you," Lyons said.

"Excellent. Let's see if he's got his phone switched on, shall we?" Lorcan said with a slightly evil grin.

He called Hays' number.

* * *

Hays was at his desk in the Galway station when his phone came to life. He looked at the screen and saw that it was Maureen Lyons calling.

"Hi. What's up?" he said cheerfully.

"I'll tell ya what's up buddy, so listen carefully. This is Lorcan McFadden. I've got your girl here with me now, and she's, well let's say, tied up at the moment. Now if you want to see her in one piece again, you'll get together ten thousand euro in used notes and wait for my next call. See ya, Mick!" He hung up and turned Lyons' phone off. He didn't want anyone phoning back that might give them the ability to trace their location.

Hays got up from his desk and moved quickly out of his office. He saw Sally Fahy and John O'Connor in the open plan and summoned them to his room urgently.

Hays explained the situation to the two Gardaí.

"First thing we need is a location. John, will you call Flynn's phone. McFadden didn't mention anything about Eamon, so maybe he's got away, although I suspect he would have been in touch if that were the case. Nevertheless, call it."

"Sally, can you get onto the Gardaí in Cavan? Lyons and Flynn should be back in the Republic by now. See if there are any reports of anything odd going down around there. Tell them a female officer's life is in danger. And then we're driving out there, so get a couple of spare phones and some other essentials and be ready to roll in ten minutes."

Hays realised that he had to maintain a professional approach in the situation but inside, his feelings were in turmoil. He had grown to love Maureen Lyons over the past couple of years, and he couldn't bear to think of her being harmed by that little scum bag McFadden. He also knew that Maureen was a fighter. She wouldn't just collapse in submission whatever was going on, and McFadden wasn't all that clever, so he felt that she would probably be OK, but he was not at all certain. McFadden's situation had gone from bad to worse, and he was getting to the point where he had little or nothing to lose, so he was almost certainly desperate. Desperate men don't normally make good decisions.

When they were on the road, Fahy told Hays that there were no reports of anything strange in the Cavan area so far, but that the sergeant in Cavan had promised to let them know immediately if anything came in.

"Do you think she'll be OK, boss?" Fahy asked the inspector.

"Inspector Lyons is extremely resourceful, Sally. She's clearly in a bad spot just now, but I'd have every faith that she'll be able to manage whatever comes along. Let's hope so anyway," he said, more in an effort to convince himself than anything else.

A moment later, Sally Fahy's mobile rang, and she answered it on speaker phone.

"This is Sergeant Dillon from Cavan calling. We have reports of a car hijacking coming in from a few miles outside the town. A woman was stopped by a female Garda, and her car was taken off her by a young man leaving her at the roadside. We have a patrol car on its way, and there seems to be another car involved in some way. It's not clear yet, but the squad car will be there within five minutes," Dillon said.

"Sergeant, this is Senior Inspector Mick Hays from Galway. The female officer is Inspector Maureen Lyons, and she has been kidnapped by the man who hijacked the car. Can you circulate details of the vehicle that was taken? And as soon as your folks get to the scene, I want an immediate report. There may be another one of our officers involved."

"Yes sir, of course. I'll call you back as soon as we have anything," Dillon replied.

"Good man. We're on our way, and should be there within the hour," Hays said, and hung up.

"Can't you get a bit more speed out of this old heap Sally, we're barely breaking the speed limit!"

"Right, sir, hold tight!"

Fahy brought the Hyundai up to 150kph, and with the blue lights and sirens made short work of the small amount of traffic that they encountered on the road.

"I'm going to call the Super. See if we can get the helicopter up. McFadden won't have gone far with Maureen," Hays said.

Superintendent Plunkett listened to Mick Hays as he outlined the situation.

"Christ, Mick, this thing goes from bad to worse. Just tell me what you want. And don't hold back," the superintendent said.

"Thanks, boss. I want a Garda helicopter up over the spot where the car was hijacked. They can liaise with Sergeant Dillon in Cavan, and if we can get the PSNI to put their bird up, so much the better. I want roadblocks on every road within ten kilometres of the hijack location, and I want two dog teams sent up there. Then, any derelict buildings in the area need to be searched. Oh, and can you get ten grand in used notes prepared in case we have to go through with the exchange?" Hays said.

"Consider it done Mick. Oh, and Mick – don't worry, we'll get her back. I haven't lost an officer yet in thirty-two years on the job."

"Thanks, boss."

* * *

McFadden used the handcuffs that had previously been around his own wrists to secure Lyons to a sturdy piece of rusting farm machinery inside the abandoned barn. He stuffed some old cloth into her mouth to stop her screaming, and settled down on a hay bale to develop the next part of his plan.

He was sure that the Gardaí would happily pay out ten thousand euro to get one of their own back in one piece, and that would be enough to get him away to

England where he could lie low for a few months and put all this behind him.

But he would need to be careful about how he secured the cash and made his escape. He couldn't very well drive out of there in the stolen car – there would be roadblocks all over the place, and he would need a vehicle to make good his getaway. So, firstly, he needed another car: something that wouldn't draw attention to itself in these parts, and if he could find one with Northern Ireland plates, all the better. He could see a farmyard about half a kilometre away from the old barn and decided to set out and have a look to see what he might find.

He was happy that Lyons was secured – with her hands cuffed to the old machine, and with her feet bound, she wasn't going anywhere.

Taking Lyons' phone with him, Lorcan set off on foot across the fields towards the farmyard.

* * *

As soon as McFadden had left, Lyons assessed her situation objectively. Clearly, she needed to get out of the cuffs and free herself if she was to escape, but it wasn't going to be easy. She managed to eject the cloth from her mouth handily enough, but decided not to start shouting as, more than likely, all that it would achieve would be to bring McFadden back, and he wouldn't be best pleased.

With feet bound, and hands out of commission, it wasn't going to be a simple job to get free. There was however a good lot of old scrap and rusty iron lying about, and she calculated that if she could somehow use her bound feet to manoeuvre a bar of the rusty metal up towards her hands, she might be able to lever the cuffs away from their mountings.

She wriggled and squirmed and finally managed to find a loose piece of iron that she thought might be useful. She scrabbled about with her bound feet, slowly but surely edging the iron bar towards her hands. She pulled at the cuffs, straining to get a grip on the bar. Her wrists were hurting a lot, and red welts were forming where they were rubbing against the metal.

After more than half an hour, she finally had the bar in her hands, and inserted it in between the handcuffs and the piece of machinery that was anchoring them. Now she needed some serious leverage to break open the cuffs.

By contorting herself, and by bringing her knees up close to her face, she managed to get the iron bar under her left leg, and then using the weight of her entire body, she leant down on it. As she put pressure on the bar, the handcuff dug deep into her wrist, and for a moment she felt that the bone might break before the cuff. With one final heave, blotting out the pain as best she could, there was a satisfying snap, and the handcuff sprang open.

"Thank God for Yoga classes!!" she said to herself.

A few minutes later she had untethered her bound ankles and was able to use her free hand with the same iron bar to break off the second handcuff. She was free, although quite exhausted and sore from all the straining and heaving.

What to do now? She could, of course, head off. It would have to be on foot, as McFadden had taken the keys of the hijacked car with him. Lyons felt that this was not the best plan, after all, she was quite likely to bump into McFadden as she made her escape, and such an encounter was unlikely to end well for her.

No. She decided to re-arrange things to look like she was still captive, and she hid her trusty, and now proven, iron bar underneath her so that she could use it as a weapon when McFadden returned.

* * *

Lorcan McFadden had no luck at the farmyard. There was a car, but it was an old Toyota, and while the keys were in it, it would obviously be missed as soon as he took it, so that was not an option. From the farmyard though, McFadden spotted another enterprise just a few hundred metres down the track. There was a modest bungalow with a huge steel shed that had a large concrete apron in front of it. There were a number of vehicles parked on the concrete in various stages of repair and decay. There didn't seem to be anyone around, so McFadden approached the site with caution. If anyone challenged him, he could say he was looking for a mate that he thought worked around there.

In the yard, he spotted an old Mercedes G Wagon in black, and as luck would have it, a Northern Ireland registration. It looked to be in roadworthy condition, with air in the tyres, and only a light covering of dust and mould on the windows and bodywork. Making his way under the cover of the other vehicles, he worked himself round to the side of the G Wagon, and gently tried the driver's door, which, as it turned out, was not locked. Inside the car, there was a pile of old rags, a few oil-stained newspapers, and a small collection of oil-covered engine parts. It was impossible to say if they belonged to this vehicle or not, so he needed to find out if the old Mercedes was driveable. Keeping a sharp eye out for anyone around, he pulled the plastic covering off the binnacle at the back of the steering wheel and found the ignition wires. Nervously, he pulled the wires free and touched the two starter wires together. There were sparks, which was good, as it confirmed that the car had a live battery. After a few sluggish heaves, the old motor coughed into life, and McFadden sat into the seat properly, and drove out of the yard. Looking in the rear-view mirror, he saw no one in pursuit.

He drove the old jeep at a fair pace till he was well out of sight of the house where it had been languishing, and then pulled off the road into a narrow, wooded lane. He took Lyons' phone out of his pocket and called the number for Mick.

Hays answered almost immediately.

"Hays," he barked into the phone.

"Hiya, Mick. Now here's your instructions. At seven o'clock I'm gonna text you a set of GPS co-ordinates. One hour later, exactly, you're to drop a bag containing ten thousand euro from a helicopter, on the exact spot. You'll be in the chopper. Then you and the chopper bugger off. When I have the money, I'll call you to tell you where your inspector can be found. If anything goes wrong, you'll never see her again." Then he hung up.

When he had finished the call, McFadden drove the old black jeep away from the site of his earlier crash, till he came to a small village with a petrol station and a Centra shop. Looking carefully around for any sign of a Garda presence, he parked a little way from the filling station, and walked to it. In the shop he bought a couple of pre-packed sandwiches, two cans of Coke and a chocolate bar. He figured Lyons might be getting peckish, and he needed somewhere to hide up until later in any case.

He then drove back to the old barn where he had left Lyons and drove the G Wagon in beside the car they had used earlier.

Lyons appeared to be asleep, lying awkwardly up against the old rusting machinery where he had left her. She feigned waking up and turned to face him.

"C'mon sleeping beauty, I've brought you some grub," McFadden called to her, nudging her shoulder.

"About time. I'm starving," she replied.

McFadden opened one of the sandwiches and leaned in towards Lyons so that she could take it from him with one of her cuffed hands. She knew she would have to time her next move to perfection. Her judgement was good, and with one fluid movement of her arm, the iron bar she had hidden underneath her body flew at McFadden's face. There was a sickening crack as two of his teeth smashed to pieces in his mouth, and the sharp end of the iron went on to gouge a deep furrow in the side of his face which immediately started to pump blood.

McFadden reeled backwards, his hand flying to his face, which was, as he realised half a second later, a mistake. Lyons still had a good grip on the iron bar, and as McFadden fell backwards with the entire front of his torso exposed, Lyons whipped around and with as much force as she could muster, drove the iron as hard as she could directly into his groin.

McFadden let out an almighty wail as he instinctively doubled up, but unfortunately for him, Lyons wasn't finished yet. As he tumbled past her, howling in agony, she bashed him firmly on the back of the head, and rendered him unconscious.

"Fuck you, McFadden," she said, "I don't even like chicken and stuffing sandwiches!"

Lyons then spent the next ten minutes trussing up the broken form of Lorcan McFadden. She bound his hands and feet and tied a ligature round his neck which she fastened to another piece of old farm machinery so that if he came around he wouldn't be able to move without choking himself.

She then went through his pockets and retrieved her phone.

"What is it this time?" Hays barked down the phone when it rang a few seconds later.

"That's a nice way to speak to a fellow inspector, sir!" she said.

"Jesus, Maureen. Thank God. Are you OK? Where's McFadden?"

"Yeah, I'm fine. Just having a sandwich and a can of Coke. McFadden's a bit tied up just now, but you can probably talk to him later. Are you going to come and get us?"

"Of course we are. Send your location using the phone and Google Maps. I'll be there as soon as we can get to you. Is McFadden secured?"

"Eh, yeah, you could say that. He's lost a few teeth, and his manhood is a bit bruised to say the least, but I think he'll live, for a day or two anyway."

"Christ, Maureen. You had us all spooked there for a while. I was thinking the worst. Send the location. We're on our way," Hays said, unable to disguise the relief he felt.

* * *

Fifteen minutes later two white 4x4s with sirens wailing and lights flashing turned into the yard where the old barn was located. Hays hopped out and ran into the barn. He couldn't believe the sight that met his eyes. There was Lyons, calm as you like, sitting on a hay bale, relaxed and smiling, and nearby, the wreck of Lorcan McFadden, with dried blood caked on his face, lips swollen, and a distant look in his eyes with his head lolling about against the ligature around his neck, barely conscious and muttering obscenities.

On the way back to Cavan in the Armed Response Unit vehicle, Lyons brought Hays fully up to date on the events of the day, from the time they collected McFadden in the North, to the time she had been found in the barn.

"He had demanded ten thousand euro for your release. He wanted it dropped by helicopter," Hays said.

"Cheeky bugger, if I'd known that was all the value he put on me, I would have given him a few more goes of the iron bar," Lyons said.

"Well you're worth a hundred times that to me, Maureen," Hays said.

"Probably not the way you would have done it, but it worked all the same," she said.

"How's Eamon by the way? He looked to be in pretty bad shape after the car crash," Lyons said.

"He's OK. They got to him pretty quickly when you two made off in the old lady's car. He's a bit concussed, and he has a broken wrist, but other than that, he's fine. He'll be as right as rain in a few days. He was very worried about you though. Blames himself for what happened," Hays said.

"Na, there's no point in that. He didn't do anything wrong. Anyway, we have another pile of charges to lay at

Mr McFadden's door now as a result. He'll be going away for a very, very long time indeed," she said.

"Right. But don't forget, we still have the Craigue kidnap to solve. McFadden was just a bit player, and Eddie Turner isn't saying much. Not yet anyway. Maybe we could show him photos of the bruising to McFadden's privates and tell him you are going to interview him – that might loosen his tongue."

* * *

When Hays and Lyons eventually got back to their house in Salthill, they were both exhausted. They sat closely together on the sofa in the lounge for half an hour to relax, and Hays cracked open a bottle of red wine. When Maureen had finished her first glass, she lay back, nestled up against her partner, and tears began to flow down her cheeks. Hays held her close.

"It's OK love, it's all over now. You did very well, you know. I can't imagine what would have happened if McFadden had got his money. You managed to close out that possibility very nicely."

"God, Mick, I'm sorry. But I was really scared. He had a wild look in his eyes, and by that time he had nothing to lose. Anything could have happened," she said.

"But you see he made one fatal mistake, didn't he? He didn't take account of the 'Lyons factor'. It's not the first time you've brought one of these toe-rags down to earth with a bang all on your own, and it may not be the last if I know you," Hays said.

"Oh don't, Mick. I think I might go back to handing out parking tickets for a while. C'mon, let's go to bed. We have another long day ahead tomorrow. I'm looking forward to bringing McFadden before a judge with a nice long rap sheet!"

Chapter Nineteen

When the two inspectors arrived at Mill Street Garda station the following day, Maureen Lyons was met with a round of applause from the rest of the team.

She was embarrassed and diverted attention from her own achievements by asking how Eamon Flynn was doing.

"They sent him home last night. His arm is in plaster, and he's a bit battered and bruised, but he's OK. He was asking for you, Inspector Lyons," John O'Connor said.

"I'm fine, thanks. Now let's get on. We have a lot to do today," she said.

John O'Connor was assigned the task of accompanying McFadden to court. They were charging him initially with two counts of causing death by dangerous driving, and two counts of assaulting a police officer in the execution of their duty. As he had already proved to be a flight risk, the Gardaí were fairly sure he would be remanded in custody until such time as they could prepare the book of evidence. If the judge made any comment about the various injuries on the prisoner's face, he was to tell the court that his injuries were sustained in the course of conducting the crimes, and during his arrest. They would leave the other charges such as vehicle theft and kidnap until later, but O'Connor was to make it clear to the court that there were further charges expected.

"That should stitch him up for a few months," Hays said.

Hays found a new file on his desk when he went into his office. It contained quite extensive details about Eddie Turner, and his life living on the margins in London, as well as details of his known associates in the big city.

Turner lived at a house at Selbourne Drive in Hendon, North London. It was a modest semi-detached residence when Hays looked it up on Google Maps, with an arch over the front door, a tiled pitched roof, pebble dashing to the front of the property, and an overgrown garden full of weeds and very long grass between the front of the house and the street.

Turner's past was peppered with a variety of infringements. He had a number of charges for burglary, and a few cases of 'taking without consent'. Buried deep in the text Hays came across a reference to a forgery charge. It hadn't stuck, but there was a case number and a few scant details showing that Turner had been found in possession of forged labels for high-end perfume products, but the CPS hadn't pursued the matter as they felt it wasn't serious enough, and the chances of a conviction were slender.

Hays called Lyons into his office.

"Here's the file on our bagman, Eddie Turner. I interviewed him yesterday and he was being very shy. He didn't give me anything. So I got onto a contact in the Met and she's sent over the file," he said, pointing to the paperwork on his desk.

"It makes interesting reading. Have a look."

"Hmm. No sign of anything too serious here, Mick. Seems a bit of a lightweight to me. But it's good to have the background. Doesn't look to me as if he's the brains behind this caper, to be honest. There's more to it. We need to get him to talk. What do you reckon?" Lyons said.

"We'll need some form of leverage. I doubt if he's too bothered about McFadden, though we could bluff him a bit. Tell him McFadden has landed him right in it, that sort of thing. Fancy a good cop, bad cop round or two with him?"

"Yeah, sure. But who's the bad cop?"

"After yesterday's performance, I'd say that's down to you," Hays said.

"How did I guess", Lyons said, rolling her eyes to heaven.

* * *

"Now Eddie," Hays said as they entered the interview room, "this is Inspector Lyons. Inspector Lyons has been spending some time with your accomplice, Lorcan, but don't worry, his injuries aren't life threatening, although his manhood will take some time to recover."

"Fuck you. You can't keep me here like this. You haven't even charged me with anything," Turner growled.

"Patience, Eddie, patience. We have plenty of time for that," Hays said.

"You can't keep me in here. I want out. This is illegal," Turner said.

"Now, Eddie, don't be like that. Aren't you enjoying our famous Irish hospitality? I wouldn't be too keen to get back to Selbourne Drive just yet if I were you. Some of your friends might not be too pleased to see you," Lyons spoke for the first time.

"And if I have a word upstairs and mention that I think there might be a subversive connection to all this stuff, then, my friend, you will be with us for a very long time indeed," Hays said.

"So, Eddie, why don't we have a nice relaxed chat, and you can tell us who exactly is behind the kidnap, and subsequent killing of Jeremy Craigue," Hays went on.

"Killing! What are you talking about. Nobody killed the lad."

"Well, I'm afraid that's not true, Eddie. I can assure you Jeremy Craigue is unfortunately very dead. Why do you think we filled the bag with torn up newspaper? Your threat to kill the boy was an empty one. He was already dead, and you're a part of that, so you could be facing a murder charge here, that's not to mention the girl," Lyons said.

"Girl, what girl?"

"Well as you know, McFadden had a girl to help him kidnap Craigue, and now she's dead as well. So that's two deaths you're involved with, as well as a string of other crimes," Hays said.

Eddie remained silent for a few moments. He looked very worried, and wriggled restlessly in his seat, rubbing his stubbly chin with his hands.

"Look. I can't tell you anything about this gig. I just can't. If I grass on the guys that set this up, I'm dead meat. I'm probably dead anyways by now, but if I stay shtum I might just be OK. So, sorry guys, you'll get nothing more from me." He sat back in the chair and folded his arms.

"OK, Eddie. We can play it your way if you like, can't we, Inspector Lyons?"

"Yes, sure, no problem. Tell you what. Why don't we release Eddie here – in fact we'll do better than that – we can give him a police escort back to Hendon, and we'll let it be known that he's done a deal with us to give up the brains in exchange for his own freedom," Lyons said.

"Good idea," Hays said, "we can ask DCI Russell to give us a hand putting out the good word."

At the mention of the senior Met officer, Eddie flinched.

"OK, let's go and make the arrangements upstairs. We should have you out of here by nightfall, Eddie," Lyons said.

"Wait." Eddie said.

"What for, Eddie? You've said that you're not going to tell us anything," Lyons said.

"OK. I'll give you the information you're looking for. But you'll have to protect me. As soon as I open my mouth my life is in danger."

Over the next hour Eddie led Hays and Lyons a merry dance. He talked endlessly about his previous misdemeanours, and his fractious relationship with the Metropolitan Police over several years. But in all his hollow wanderings he never once mentioned a name or gave any hint of who had masterminded the kidnap of Jeremy Craigue.

Eventually the Gardaí got fed up with the man and brought the interview to an end.

Back in their office, Hays said that all they could do for now, other than start the process of charging the Englishman, was to get back onto DCI Russell and see if she could give them any more assistance. Hays said that he would have to go upstairs to update Superintendent Plunkett, and when he got back he would make the call.

"Is there something I should know about you and the fragrant DCI Russell?" Lyons said.

"What? Oh no. We worked together a few years back on some terrorist cases. She's always been very helpful, but it's purely professional – always was."

Hays was back a few minutes later.

"What did the Super say?" Lyons said.

"He's not terribly interested to be honest. He wants us to make sure the Craigues are OK, give them any assistance that we can. Oh, and he asked about McFadden. He wanted to make sure he didn't get bail and we had enough to keep him indoors for a good few years," Hays said.

"No worries on that score. Now I suppose you want me to drive all the way out to bloody Ballyconneely again?" Lyons said.

"Hmm. I have a better idea. Why don't we both go out to see them. And let's bring that list of Eddie's known associates with us, see if anyone on the list rings a bell with Bernard," Hays said.

"Not just a pretty face, are you?" she said, smiling.

Chapter Twenty

It was a warm summer's day as the two senior Gardaí drove out west from Galway city. The weather was holding up unusually well. Once they were beyond Oughterard, the true beauty of the place took over. The boggy heathland, resplendent in the mauve colour of the early heathers, contrasted strikingly with the yellow of the gorse bushes all along the edge of the roadside. In the distance, the mountains created a magnificent backdrop to the picture postcard scene.

"What are we going to do with McFadden? Do you think he has any more to give us?" Lyons said.

"Hard to tell. What do you think? You have a nose for this kind of thing," Hays replied.

"I don't think he has to be honest, but I think we could use him all the same. Play him off against Turner. But I'm sure he hasn't a clue who Turner answers to."

As they passed Recess, Hays said, "Can you go in via Roundstone? Do you mind?"

"No problem. What do you want to see?"

"I just want to spend a few minutes at Dog's Bay, maybe walk the beach. Clear my head a bit."

"Oh, OK. Not a bad idea. What time did you tell the Craigues we would be out there?" Lyons asked.

"That's not a problem. They said anytime today, they're not going anywhere till Jeremy's body is released. Then they'll be off back to the UK."

When they had passed through Roundstone village they drove a further mile or so until they reached the little lane that led down to the beach. They turned in and drove slowly down the bumpy track to the car park just beyond the entrance to the old abandoned caravan site. As Hays parked the car at a ninety-degree angle to the coastline, the brilliant blue of the clear sea with the sun glinting on it and the waves lapping gently on the white sand made a magnificent sight.

They both got out of the car and inhaled deeply. The scent of the grass and the clear sea air was exhilarating, and they strolled over to the little wicket gate that gave them access to the beautiful horseshoe shaped beach. The beach was actually comprised of crushed sea shells that had been ground very finely by the constant ebb and flow of the Atlantic ocean smashing them against the rocks. A few years back, erosion had threatened the area, and Galway County Council had responded by importing marram grass that would root in the sand, and prevent the wind from blowing it away. Their efforts had been very successful, and the beach and the stunning heathland with its picturesque dunes were now preserved for the locals and visitors to enjoy.

As soon as they were on the strand, Hays took Maureen's hand in his, and they strolled silently out towards the headland, leaving their footsteps in the sand behind them.

"Penny for them," Lyons said when they had walked half way across towards the promontory.

"I was just thinking about you – us really. I reacted very badly to that nonsense you were caught up in with McFadden. All sorts of images invaded my thoughts, none of them very pleasant. You do know that I love you, Maureen, very much, don't you?" Hays said.

She turned to face him, and they kissed warmly for a long time, just standing there on the beach in each other's arms with no one else at all around to see them.

When they parted from the kiss, she snuggled into his chest, and looking up at him, said softly, "And I thought you were going off me a bit. You know. I got the feeling you thought I'd made a mess of things out here on the first day when you were out on your boat. I got the impression you felt you would have done things much better than I did, and you were pissed off with me for being a plonker."

"Oh God, Maureen. You're no plonker. I don't have plonkers in my team, you know that. And look how you dealt with McFadden. If you hadn't tackled him with your trusty iron bar, he'd have been away to England with ten thousand euro of Irish tax payers' money up his jumper. And God knows what he would have done to you."

"Yeah, I know. I was pretty scared to be honest. It's not nice dealing with violent criminals who have nothing to lose. But once my self-preservation instincts kicked in, his days were numbered. I'm not giving in to the likes of him that easily, that's for sure," she said.

They walked further out along the strand, this time with their arms around each other, closer to each other, enjoying the warmth of their love and the sun that was beating down on the landscape.

"Would you fight like that to keep me, if you had to?" Hays said.

"Unfair question, and hopefully a situation that will never arise – but if it does, you'll find out then just how tough Inspector Maureen Lyons can be. You ain't seen nothing yet!"

"God help us all! C'mon. Let's go and see these poor people, see what we can find out," he replied.

* * *

"Thank you for seeing us, Mr Craigue, I know this is difficult for you," Hays said as they were shown into the lounge with the magnificent view out over the beach.

"Just to bring you up to date, we now have two men in custody that we believe were involved in your son's abduction. But we believe there may be some others involved as well. The two we have aren't able to give us any information about the real motive for the kidnap, other than the money of course, but we believe that there may be another dimension to it. I wonder if I could ask you to look at this list of names and see if any of them are familiar to you?" Lyons said.

She handed Bernard Craigue the sheet of paper that listed Eddie Turner's known associates which they had received from the Metropolitan Police, and watched carefully as he looked at it.

"No, I can't say I recognize any of those names. I'm sorry," he said, handing it back to her.

"I know this is difficult, Mr Craigue, but are you certain?" Hays said.

"Yes, I'm certain. None of them are familiar to me."

"Well, thanks for looking anyway. May I ask what your immediate plans are?" Hays said.

"As soon as you can release Jeremy's body…" He stopped for a moment, overcome with emotion, "we'll be heading back to London. Hannah's sister is coming over to be with us for the journey. It's just too sad," the man said, and broke down again.

"Would you like us to get the police in London to assign a family liaison officer? They can be a great help in these circumstances," Lyons said.

"I'll talk to Hannah about it and let you know. Maybe that would be useful. Will we need to come back here at any stage? To be honest, we've gone right off the place since this happened. We'll probably sell up as soon as we get things sorted out."

"I see. If I could offer some advice, Mr Craigue, don't do anything too hastily. You might feel differently in a month or two, and you'll never get a house like this again in these parts," Hays said.

"We'll see," he said, standing up.

"Well thank you for your time, Mr Craigue. We'll be in touch as soon as Jeremy's body can be released. It shouldn't be much longer."

Back in the car, heading for Clifden so that they could take the quicker road back into Galway, Hays asked Lyons what she thought.

"I can't be certain, but I think he recognised someone on the list. I was watching him very carefully as he read down through it, and I noticed his eyes flare for an instant when he was near the end. Just a flicker, but I spotted it all the same," Lyons said.

"Really? Are you sure you didn't imagine it?"

"Well I definitely saw it, but then I have a suspicious mind in any case," she said.

* * *

Eddie Turner had been brought back to the interview room for a second round of questioning.

"Well now, Eddie, now that you have had time to reflect on your situation, we just thought we'd have another little chat. Tell us, Eddie, what were your plans for the 100,000 euros? That's a lot of money for a fella to come into all of a sudden," Hays said.

"No comment."

"Now, Eddie, I hope you're not going to start that again. I'm not sure you realise just how bad your situation is here. Our superintendent wants us to throw the book at you. That means you'll be our guest here in Ireland for a good few years. You'll probably end up in Limerick Prison, and I can tell you, Eddie, they're not too fond of Englishmen down there. Quite a few have come to a sticky end in that dump," Lyons said.

"Are you threatening me?" Turner said.

"Of course not, Eddie. Just telling you how it is, that's all. However, if you were to co-operate with us, it could be very different. You'll still do time, but we could arrange a much more friendly billet for you, and it wouldn't be that long in any case. But we need you to give us some information."

"What sort of information?"

"We need to know who is behind this whole caper. Who's pulling your strings, Eddie? Just a name is all we need. We can do the rest, and we won't be saying who told us either," Lyons said.

"I can't. They'd kill me quick as wink. I'm saying nothing." He folded his arms across his chest.

"OK. Well there is another way we could do this, Eddie," Hays said. "Your friends will be wondering where you've got to with the hundred grand. 'Spose you were to give them a call to tell them that you'd been nicked, and the whole thing went pear-shaped. Tell them the boy is dead too. We could just listen in while you make the call."

"You think I'm fucking thick! No chance."

"Tell you what, Eddie. Why don't you take a bit of time to think about things? We'll be back later, and if you haven't decided to help us, then we'll start putting the wheels in motion to have you charged and brought before a judge. Remind me, Maureen, what charges we have for Eddie here," Hays said.

"Let's see. Well there's kidnap, extortion, conspiracy, assaulting a police officer, oh… and, of course, accessory to murder, and that's just for starters," Lyons said

"Murder. I didn't do no murder. That's bollocks," Eddie protested.

"Eddie. Wake up. We have two dead bodies on our hands and we have McFadden in custody. Now someone has to go down for these deaths, and you look like just the man for the job, so think on," Hays said, getting up to leave.

* * *

Back at his desk, Hays got a message that the superintendent was looking for him. Picking up the phone he dialled Plunkett's number.

"Ah, Mick. Thanks for getting back to me. I hear you have two in custody for that fiasco out in Roundstone. Good work," Plunkett said.

"Thanks, sir. Yes, we have a couple of suspects, but that's not the end of it. There's a UK connection that we need to flush out to wrap it up."

"Are you sure that's the best use of our time, Mick? If we have the two lads, isn't that enough for us?"

"Well I'd like to see it through, sir. These boys are just the infantrymen, I'm looking for the generals."

"That's all very well, Mick, but we have to be careful how we use our resources these days. I'd be just as happy to see this whole thing wrapped up to be honest, and there's no shame if we have enough to put our two heroes away for a few years."

"I understand, sir. But can you give me a couple more days pursuing enquiries, and if I don't get anywhere, then we'll call it a day?"

"All right, Mick. Let me know if there are any developments."

"That went well then," Lyons said.

"We'll have to stitch this up in the next two or three days or he'll go nuts. And we need a result as well. Why don't you get back onto DCI Russell in the Met and see if she can do a bit more digging for us. I've a feeling the mastermind behind all this is on that list."

Back at her own desk, Lyons called DCI Russell in Scotland Yard. When she had introduced herself, she went on to ask Russell for some further help.

"We were wondering if you could help us find out a bit more about Eddie Turner's known associates. Inspector Hays thinks there's a definite link there to the people behind this, and he's anxious to bring them in if he can," she said.

"I'm sorry, Inspector Lyons, but I simply can't afford to put any more time into this for you. We're up to our eyes here just now," the chief inspector said.

"Oh, right. That's a shame. You see if we could nab whoever is behind this, it would probably make your life a bit easier too. One less villain to worry about on your patch."

"I see what you mean. I'll tell you what… Now this mustn't go any further, it's more than my career is worth. Have you got a spare burner phone handy?" Russell said.

"Eh, not just here, but I can get one easily enough," Lyons said.

"OK. Well when you have it, call me back with the number. I'm going to send you a link to one of our systems. You'll be able to log in over the internet, but for God's sake use a proxy server in the UK. That will give you access to everything we have on these blokes, but if you tell anyone about it, I'll have to shoot you. Oh, and I'll be changing the password tonight, so you'll have to do whatever you need to today."

"That's terrific, Inspector, thank you. I'll treat it with respect, don't worry."

Lyons wasted no time in slipping out to the nearest phone shop and buying a cheap pay-as-you-go phone. Back in her office, after she had unwrapped it and put it on to charge, she called DCI Russell back with the number.

A few minutes later her new phone pinged, and Lyons opened the text message. It contained a www.metsafe999.co.uk hyperlink.

Lyons then asked John O'Connor if he could set up a PC using a UK proxy, so that she could connect to the web site Russell had given her and make it look as if she was located in the UK.

"That's no problem, Inspector, give me ten minutes and I'll have it set up. I assume you want to be totally anonymous?"

"Definitely John, can you fix that up?"

"Sure. I can use the little phone you just bought as a hotspot. I'll tether a PC to it, and then we can destroy it as soon as you've finished on the site and no one will ever be able to trace it."

Lyons hadn't a clue what he was talking about but trusted him to ensure that she would be able to use the link without getting either herself or DCI Russell into trouble.

Lyons gave the list that they had previously received from DCI Russell to John O'Connor when he had finished setting up the PC.

"John, I want you to go through this list using the database and get me as much information as you can on each of the names. If these names link to other names, get the low down on them too. Print the details off as you go, and make sure you don't leave any traces behind you. And you'll need to work quickly, we don't have a lot of time."

"No problem, boss. Any chance I could get Sally to help me? She's good at this kind of thing."

"Yes, of course. But be sure to swear her to secrecy. If it was revealed that we had this link it could cause a major diplomatic kerfuffle!" Lyons said.

Lyons relayed the information to Hays who was delighted with the support coming from London, and the way Lyons had handled the whole thing.

"That's great. Let's see what comes up," he said.

Chapter Twenty-one

Sergeant Séan Mulholland started his trawl through various sets of records in search of information on Sheila O'Rourke, the girl that had died in such forlorn circumstances after McFadden had crashed the getaway car. He started with the Department of Social Welfare, and followed a trail of obscure references till eventually he had a more or less complete picture of Sheila's family and some insight into her circumstances.

Sheila was one of two girls, the other being five years younger than her, and she had been born to Marie and Liam O'Rourke in 2001. Sheila's parents had married in 1999 and Sheila had come along just over a year later. There was nothing untoward recorded in their history. Liam was a PAYE worker in a factory on the Ballybritt estate just outside Galway, and Marie worked in administration for the local authority in the city. They lived in a modest semi-detached house in Ardilaun Park on the outskirts of Galway, and were, according to the records Mulholland was able to consult, Catholic.

In 2010 Liam developed cancer, and was in and out of Galway Regional Hospital for just over a year till the disease finally claimed him, his death occurring in 2012, by which time the O'Rourkes had added another daughter, Amy, to the family.

The next appearance in the records was the re-marriage of Marie O'Rourke to a Pat Bolger, a previously unmarried man from Galway. Mr and Mrs Bolger, the newly-weds, had retained the O'Rourke family house in Ardilaun Park, and as far as Mulholland could tell were living there to this day.

When Mulholland had as much information as he felt he needed, he telephoned Sally Fahy to share it with her.

"That's great, Sergeant. I'll see what they want to do here. There's no point you driving all the way in from Clifden just to give them the bad news," Sally said.

When she relayed the information to Hays, her worst fears were realised.

"OK Sally, thanks. I'd like you to go round there and break the bad news to the girl's mother. Are you OK with that?" Hays said.

"Well, I guess so. Could I take someone with me? I haven't done this before," she said.

"Yes, of course. Bring a uniformed Garda, oh and go in an unmarked car. We don't want to make a show of the Bolgers."

* * *

When Sally knocked at the door of the Bolger's house, it was answered by a young girl of about twelve who had apparently just arrived back from school, as she was still wearing her green school skirt and matching green jumper with a white blouse and a red hairband in her long dark brown hair.

"Is your mother in?" Sally said.

The girl said nothing, but turned her back on the two officers and went back into the house shouting, "Mum, it's for you," and promptly disappeared.

Marie Bolger appeared at the door a few seconds later. Marie was a woman in her mid to late forties, with short, dyed blonde hair, brushed back at the sides of her head. She was around 5'4" in height, and a little plump. She was dressed in grey leggings, with a floral top – an outfit which didn't do much to flatter her – but Sally could still see where Sheila had got her looks.

Sally introduced herself and her uniformed assistant, and asked if they might come in for a moment.

Marie Bolger showed them into the front room of the house, which was decorated in a rather dated style, with a dark brown sofa and green patterned wallpaper that was none too fresh. Nevertheless, the room was clean, as were the windows, and the two Gardaí were happy to take a seat, while Marie sat in the armchair closer to the fireplace.

"How can I help you officers?" Mrs Bolger said.

"Am I right in saying that you have a daughter, Sheila, from your first marriage, Mrs Bolger?" Sally said.

"Oh that one. Oh yes, she's mine all right. What has she done now? She's nothing but trouble."

"May I ask if she's living here with you and Mr Bolger?" Sally said.

"No, she left last year. Mind you it doesn't stop her coming round pestering me for money every now and then, but I soon send her packing, I've more to be doing with the little we have. She's no good you know, never was."

"Mrs Bolger, I'm sorry to have to tell you that I believe your daughter may be no longer with us," Sally said.

"No longer with us. What do you mean? Is she dead?"

"Well, a girl named Sheila O'Rourke was involved in a road traffic accident out in Connemara, and passed away from her injuries. We think this girl may be your daughter. I'm very sorry Mrs Bolger. Is there someone we could call for you, a relative or a neighbour maybe?" Sally said.

Marie Bolger sat silently for a moment or two, remembering her daughter, and the great times that she and Liam had had with her when she was growing up. She had been a good child, full of fun, and always well behaved until Liam had passed on and Pat Bolger had come into their lives.

"There's no need for any of that. I'm fine. I always thought she'd end up in big trouble that one. She was always up to no good," Mrs Bolger said. Inwardly, her heart was breaking.

"Mrs Bolger, I'm sorry to have to ask, but can you tell me why Sheila left home last year? I understand she would have been sixteen then. That's quite young, even these days." Sally said.

"Who knows what was going on in her twisted little head, officer. One day, she just upped and went without so much as a by your leave. Left a note saying it was best for all of us that she went. That was it."

"How did she get on with Mr Bolger?" the uniformed Garda asked.

"Fine. Of course she missed her real dad, but herself and Pat seemed to get along OK. They weren't particularly close – not like Amy, she adores him," the woman said.

"I see. Well, we will need you to come to the mortuary to identify Sheila's body for us. Would tomorrow morning be convenient, when Amy is at school? We can send a car for you, and if you'd like someone with you, that's fine too," Sally said.

"Tomorrow's fine, say ten o'clock, and I'll not be bringing anyone with me."

"Oh, and we'll need to speak to Mr Bolger too at some stage. Have you got a mobile number for him?" Sally said.

"Why do you need to talk to Pat? He won't be able to tell you anything I haven't," Marie Bolger said.

"Just routine, Mrs Bolger. You wouldn't believe the amount of paperwork these things generate and we have to dot the eyes and cross the tees."

"Very well, I'll jot Pat's number down for you. You can see him after work."

When the two Gardaí had left, Marie Bolger sat at the kitchen table and wept silently. She cried for what was, and for what might have been. When Liam had died, she had been left a relatively young widow with two young girls to bring up, and only half a wage to sustain all three of them. Liam had no life assurance, but at least the mortgage on the house was paid off with his passing, so she didn't have to worry about keeping a roof over their heads.

Once she had got over Liam's death, Marie smartened herself up and made sure that she got out to social gatherings and parties, and it wasn't long before she caught the attention of Pat Bolger.

Pat was no great shakes, but he was a good earner, and at first at least, he was kind to her and the children. Their love life was adequate, not as good as it had been with Liam, but Marie knew that she had to make some sacrifices in the difficult circumstances into which she had been plunged with the death of her husband, so she settled for what was on offer. She had seen the way Pat looked at Sheila from time to time, especially when the girl would dress up in a short skirt on her way out to a disco or a party at a friend's house, but she dismissed any thoughts of impropriety. It would have been much too difficult to go there.

Chapter Twenty-two

By late afternoon, O'Connor and Fahy had printed off more than thirty pages of information. They had used the names on the list and burrowed deep into the database provided by DCI Russell to establish as many links as they could. They carried the stack of paper into where Hays was seated at his desk.

"Crikey, you've been busy. Are you still digging, or is that it?" Hays said

"That's it for now, boss. If you think any of them are worth a closer look, we can do some more," Fahy said.

"Could you ask Inspector Lyons to come in please?" he said.

Lyons and Hays took half each of the pile of sheets that Fahy had brought in and spent the next hour reading through the information. Eddie's cronies were mostly a rag-bag collection of small time villains. There were a good few who had been involved in the motor trade. One of his mates had been caught running a chop-shop down in the East End of London, and a couple of others had been involved in taking and exporting high-end motors to the Middle East.

"This looks interesting," Lyons said.

"What's that?"

"There's a Samuel Chapman here. Seems he's been connected with printing forged designer labels and boxes for luxury perfumes like Chanel. It's quite recent too."

Hays smiled, "I remember that wheeze from when I visited London years ago. They sell the stuff on Oxford Street and around Leicester Square. They have one genuine bottle of the perfume that they use to draw in the gullible punters, and a suitcase full of forgeries with nothing but yellow water. At ten quid a pop they can clear five hundred pounds in half an hour," Hays said.

"Why don't the punters, as you call them, open their purchase and smell it?" Lyons said.

"Oh, that's the clever bit. The vendor tells them it's stolen gear, and they had better hide it away in their shopping bag till they get home," Hays said.

"Cute. Sounds like you were had," Lyons said, smirking.

"No comment." Hays replied.

"Well this Chapman fella was caught with a whole garage full of printed labels and boxes for various expensive brands. It wasn't his first offence either. He got eighteen months for forgery, but only served half. He was released about two months ago," Lyons said.

"Why do you think he might be important?" Hays said.

"Dunno. Just a feeling, and the obvious printing connection. Wasn't Bernard Craigue in that line before he retired?"

"I think he was, you're right. It's a bit tenuous, but let's ask Sally to go back into the database while we still have access and do a deep dive on Chapman," he said.

* * *

When they arrived at the Craigues' house the following morning the weather had changed dramatically. The wind was blowing hard in from the sea carrying a fine spray, and overhead thick grey clouds reached right down to skim the hill tops as they scurried past.

Inside the bungalow, large cardboard boxes were scattered throughout the hall and lounge. Pictures had been taken down off the walls, and bookshelves that had previously been laden with popular fiction and books about the west of Ireland, were now bare and forlorn looking.

"We're packing up," said Bernard Craigue. "We're taking our stuff back to London, and we're going to put this place up for sale. Hannah says she can't be here anymore. Too many memories."

"Sorry to hear that, Mr Craigue, but it's perfectly understandable. We were just wondering if we could clarify a few things with you?" Lyons said.

"Of course. Would you like a cup of tea or coffee? The machine is still working."

When the coffee had been brewed, the four of them sat around the kitchen table. The room was at the back of the house where the rocky land rose steeply, but even in the harsh Atlantic rain, Hays thought the view and the unique position of the property were spectacular.

"What's on your minds?" Bernard Craigue said.

"I understand you used to be in the printing business, Mr Craigue," Hays said.

"Yes, that's right. I sold up a few years back, but that was my trade."

"Did you ever come across a man by the name of Samuel Chapman?"

Craigue visibly flinched at the mention of the name. His hands jerked, and he spilled some coffee on the table.

"Why do you ask, Inspector?"

"It's just that when we were here the other day, we showed you a list of names, and Chapman was one of them, but you told us you didn't recognize any of them."

"Well I was pretty upset at the time, Inspector. My only son had just been killed."

"So you do know Chapman then?" Lyons asked.

"I used to work for a Samuel Chapman in London, but it's a long time ago now. I doubt if he would remember me," Craigue said.

Hannah Craigue got up from the table and left the room without speaking. Lyons noticed she was wringing her hands as she hurried away.

"Can you tell us a little bit more about your relationship with Mr Chapman?" Hays said.

"There's not much to tell. I worked for him for a few years. He made me up to manager, but he had a son, Peter, who was being lined up to take over the business, so I knew I wouldn't get much further. I left and started up my own printing firm," Craigue said.

"And did you part on good terms, Mr Craigue?" Lyons said.

"Oh yes, very good terms. He even said to me if it didn't work out he would take me back," Craigue said.

"But that didn't happen I presume? How long did you have your own company?" Lyons asked.

"Twelve years. I built it up quite quickly once we got going. I worked really hard for the first five years taking almost any work we could get, and then we sourced the magazine contracts. It got a lot easier from then on."

"Did you ever do any work for any of the big cosmetic companies?" Lyons said.

"No, never. Our speciality was full colour litho printing – brochures, mags, catalogues – that kind of thing. We did work for some of the fashion houses, but that's as close as we got to cosmetics. Fussy buggers they were too. Give me Woman's Way any day," he said, reminiscing.

"Do you know what became of Chapman's company after you left?" Hays said.

"Not really. I heard in the trade that it had gone down hill quite a bit, and there were rumours that he had got into some dodgy stuff lately, but I didn't pay it much heed to be honest. It's probably down to the son. That's why I sold up, you know. Second generations always make a mess of the father's business. I didn't want Jeremy to do that, and he didn't want it either," Craigue said.

Bernard Craigue's eyes filled with tears as the memory of his son came back to him. The two detectives sensed that it was the right time to leave.

Outside in the car, Hays said, "Let's head into Clifden and get some lunch. I want to phone John O'Connor in any case, and there's no signal out here."

They stopped at the Garda station in Clifden and found Jim Dolan alone behind the desk. Hays used the station's phone to call back to Mill Street. John O'Connor was at lunch, but he got speaking to Sally Fahy who never seemed to eat anything at all in the middle of the day.

"Sally, do we still have access to that UK database?" he said.

"Hold on sir, I'll check on my PC."

Hays could hear the keyboard clicking in the background.

"Sorry, sir. It looks like the password has been changed. I can't log on," she said.

"Damn. OK. Could you put a call in to DCI Russell for me? Use your Irish charm to ask her to look up one Peter Chapman and send over anything she can find. Tell her it's the last favour we will ask of her."

They drove back into the centre of Clifden and decided to have lunch at Foyle's Hotel. Luckily, they got a parking spot just outside, for the heavy shower hadn't let up, and the accompanying breeze made it feel a lot colder than the eighteen degrees reported on the car's outside temperature gauge.

They finished the delicious seafood chowder, and while they were waiting for the roast lamb main course, Lyons asked Hays, "Are you sure you and Irene Russell weren't an item at one stage then?"

"No, not at all. We had a few boozy nights out in London together, but that was it. I can't be certain, but I'm fairly sure Irene is on the other bus."

"Seriously! Jesus, that's gas. And here was me ready to do the jealous girlfriend act."

"Have you seen her photo? Very short boy-cut hair, broad shoulders, not much on top and big hips. Don't get me wrong, she's very nice, and a damn fine cop, but I don't think she's into men," Hays said.

"I won't be getting my hair cut short anytime soon then," Lyons said, smirking.

"Ah, go on. I thought you and Sally would make a lovely couple. I can just imagine …"

"Fuck off, Mick, you pervert." They both laughed out loud.

* * *

Fahy had persuaded DCI Russell to look into Peter Chapman, and when Hays and Lyons returned to the station, an A4 sheet about the man was on Hays' desk.

"Well now, young Peter has been a naughty boy," Hays said.

There were a series of minor crimes listed on the sheet that Hays had in front of him. But more importantly, at the end of the page, under 'Notes', someone had added:

"Suspected of involvement with a number of known criminals in London. Insufficient evidence to pursue at this time."

Chapter Twenty-three

On the way into work the following morning in Hays' car, Lyons said, "I was thinking about Eddie and the Chapmans last night. I have an idea."

"Oh-oh. God help them now. So, what's your idea?" Hays said.

"How would you like to snag Peter for this whole thing? He'd get a good few years, and Irene would love you forever, regardless," she said.

"Are you going to share your brainwave with me?"

"Not just yet, but you'll like it, don't fret."

"That's what I'm afraid of. Is it at least legal?" Hays said.

"Of course! Well, sort of."

* * *

Eddie Turner was brought back to the interview room as soon as they got to the Garda station. Hays had asked Lyons to conduct the interview with Eamon Flynn. Hays wanted to stay in the background for this one in case it all fell apart. This way, he could possibly rescue the situation and provide some cover for Maureen.

"Right, Eddie, we just wanted to bring you up to date with what's been happening," Lyons said.

"We've been speaking to the superintendent, and he wants the whole thing wrapped up as soon as possible. He's told us to charge you with everything we can think of and get you in front of a judge tomorrow morning."

"So, what are the charges then?" Eddie said, looking apprehensive.

"Eamon, what have we got so far?" Lyons said.

"Let's see," Flynn said, turning over a few pages in his notebook for effect, "There's kidnap of course, and extortion, then we have conspiracy to murder and perverting the course of justice, and the Super wants us to include a few 'Offences against the State' for good measure. That always gets the judges going, especially seeing as you're English."

"This is bollocks, and you know it. I ain't done half of that stuff. You're fitting me up," Turner protested.

"Well, I see what you mean, Eddie. But we have two dead bodies. We've got to make it look good in front of the judge, don't we? Of course, if you were to co-operate with us now, we might be able to see about reducing the charges, maybe even make some of it go away," Lyons said.

"How can I? I told you, I'd be signing my own death warrant. You can piss off. I'll face the music."

"It doesn't have to be like that, Eddie. What if I was to give you a way out of this with your arse intact? No repercussions. At least hear what I have to say before you reject it," Lyons said.

She looked Turner coldly in the eye and saw his pupils flare.

"Gotcha!" she said to herself.

* * *

"Is that you, Mr Chapman? It's Eddie, Eddie Turner."

Peter Chapman was in his Porsche on the M25 heading for Gatwick when the call came through. He was on his way to collect some merchandise from the cargo terminal there.

"Jesus, Eddie, where the fuck are you? And where's my money?"

"I'm in the fucking west of Ireland. The whole caper went tits up. The driver crashed the getaway car and the lad died. Total cluster fuck. But it's not all bad. The money's safe." Eddie said.

"Well that's something. When can you get back here with it?"

"That's just it, I can't. The whole place was swarming with cops when I went to pick it up. I had to hide the cash and make a run for it. I got away, but they're closing in on me now. I'm going to get lifted any second," Eddie said.

"Fuck, Eddie, you stupid bastard. So why are you calling me?" Chapman said.

"That's just it, Mr Chapman, I can't go back and collect the loot 'cos I'll be banged up. But you could come and get it," Eddie said.

"Jesus, Eddie, why have a dog and bark yourself?"

"No, it's not like that. The money is safe. But I'm not telling the cops where it is, and I'm not telling no other bugger either."

The traffic on the M25 slowed to a crawl, and Chapman was just inching along. He thought about the money, and how much 'stock' he could buy with it.

"Right, well here's what to do. Text me the location of wherever you stashed the cash. Then for fuck sake destroy that phone – and I mean completely destroy it. And if I can collect the money without incident, I might just spare your sorry ass – just maybe!" With that, he hung up.

"Well done, Eddie," Lyons said, "now give me the phone. When we have sent on the location, I'm going to cut up the SIM card in case he calls back."

Chapter Twenty-four

"John, that phone call that we just made to the UK, where did it end up?" Lyons asked.

"Hold on, boss. I'll have it in a few minutes. Yes, here it is, just coming in now. It came from a mast alongside the M25. Then it switched to another mast, further south, just past Heathrow.

"My guess is he'll wait till tomorrow to come over," Lyons said to Flynn and O'Connor. "But we need to be ready for him. It's really important, John, that you stay on top of his phone. We'll use that to track his movements, and if there's any sign of him getting here any earlier, let me know at once."

"What's the plan, boss?" Flynn said.

"The co-ordinates Eddie gave him are for an old abandoned cottage out near Murvey on the sea side of the road down by the shore. We had to direct him out near the original pick up point to make it realistic. There's only one single narrow track down to the place, so it should be easy enough to grab him. We'll need to do it just as he collects the bag though, so Sally, can you get on to Sergeant Mulholland in Clifden and get him to place a realistic looking bag down at the house. And get him to do it today," Lyons said.

"Sure, I'll do it now," the junior officer said.

"John, as soon as Chapman's phone goes near an airport, I want to know about it," Lyons said.

"OK, boss."

"Eamon, you come with me. We'd better tell Mick what's going on, he may need to brief the Super."

On the way to Hays' office, Flynn asked, "Do you think he will be armed?"

"I doubt it. He won't risk trying to smuggle a weapon on board an aircraft, and he'd hardly know where to get his hands on one over here. Besides, I doubt he perceives a threat. Eddie was quite convincing," Lyons said.

They brought Senior Inspector Mick Hays fully up to date with the new developments.

"Christ, Maureen. What did you have to promise Turner to get him to do that?" Hays asked.

"Nothing. It's what I promised him if he didn't do it that motivated him," she said.

"Don't tell me, I don't want to know. Eamon, you'd better draw up a list of all the flights from the London area to Ireland between now and tomorrow night. Then get onto the airlines. Speak to their head of security. Reassure them that there's no risk for them, we just want information quickly when we need it," Hays said.

"Right, sir. Anything else?" Flynn said.

"No. Not for now. Just make sure everyone knows we're all on call till this thing is over," he said.

Flynn left to set things up, and Hays said to Lyons, "What's your plan for when he turns up? Deasy's old red van again?" Hays said.

"Not on your life. This time we go mob handed. ARU, dogs, the lot."

* * *

Lyons' mobile phone rang.

"Inspector, it's John. Our target's phone has just been pinged on a mast at the edge of Gatwick airport. Maybe he's coming our way sooner than we thought."

"Shit. OK, quick. Get everyone together at once. I'll be down immediately," she said.

"What's up?" Hays said.

"He's only bloody well arrived at Gatwick already. C'mon, let's go," she said.

When they got to the incident room, John met them at the door.

"Sorry, boss, it could be a false alarm. His phone has logged onto another mast at the back of the airport in the village of Charlwood."

O'Connor brought up a map of the area on the big screen and pointed to a small village just past the end of the main runway at Gatwick.

"Eamon, have you got a list of flights from Gatwick to Dublin this evening?" Lyons asked.

"Yes, boss. There isn't one for four hours or so, and then that's the last one for the night."

* * *

Peter Chapman drove the Porsche around the back of the Dog and Pheasant in Charlwood. He parked beside the bins and got out of the car. He checked to see that there was no one about and walked casually over to the large blue wheelie bin. He found the package easily enough under the bin. It felt about right, and Andrei, the loader from the airport, was very reliable. He popped the plastic zip-lock bag containing 500 pounds well under the bin, got back into his car and drove off towards London.

The package Peter had collected contained a set of printing plates. Following the introduction of euro notes in 2002, the EU hadn't changed them at all, while at the same time printing technology had advanced considerably. It was now relatively easy to forge good quality fifty euro notes, and that's exactly what Peter Chapman intended to do.

The plates he had collected originated in North Korea, with the payment to the loader at Gatwick just the last in a very long chain of arrangements made to get them safely and undiscovered into his hands. It's amazing how many nooks and crannies there are on an aircraft where small items can easily be hidden away, provided you know where to look.

The Koreans were well known for their prowess in producing fake currency. Some would even say that their 'Super Dollars' were better than the real thing. The euro plates had cost Chapman a great deal of money, but he reckoned it was well spent, as it was the only currency used in so many different countries, and hence it was quite easy to pass forgeries into circulation without arousing suspicion. Anyway, he had a pretty sum due to him from the Irish caper in the near future, so in his view, it was an investment worth making.

As he drove back through the evening traffic, he thought about the team of runners that would soon be dispatched to the resorts of the Mediterranean and Aegean with their pockets stuffed full of bogus currency to be washed clean and returned to him – less expenses, of course.

* * *

Lyons studied the list of flights that Eamon had printed out. The earliest was 06:50 from Luton, followed quickly by departures from Stansted, Heathrow and Gatwick, all bound for Dublin. They had asked both the Ryanair, British Airways and Aer Lingus staff to let them know if anyone called Chapman purchased a ticket or boarded a flight for Ireland. At seven a.m. John O'Connor got a call from the Ryanair supervisor at Gatwick.

"Mr Chapman has just purchased a ticket on our nine thirty service to Knock Airport," she said. "He'll be boarding in twenty minutes."

When O'Connor relayed the message to Lyons who was still at home, she was not best pleased.

"Damn. Knock is only two hours away from Roundstone. Thanks, John, we'd better get a move on," she said.

On the way into Mill Street Garda station, Lyons called Eamon Flynn.

"Eamon, can you get onto Claremorris Gardaí? Send them over the photo of Chapman we got from the web yesterday. Tell them to get out there and watch for him. Don't let them arouse his suspicion. Ask them to confirm his arrival from Gatwick and tell us what he does next. Chances are he'll hire a car. I want the make, colour and registration number of the vehicle, but ask them not to follow him. We know where he's headed anyway, and they might get spotted," Lyons said.

When she arrived into work, Lyons gathered the team together.

"We have about two hours to get into position, and we have to do it without being seen. So civilian cars only. Sally, can you see if you can find Joe Mason. Take him and his dog out in your car. Park out of sight on the main road and hike down to the old house. There's an old shed beside the cottage itself. Get in there and stay out of sight," Lyons said.

"Eamon, you need to hook up with Mulholland and Dolan out in Clifden. Position yourselves before and after the track down to the sea at Murvey. Again, stay well out of sight, and make sure your radios are working."

Next, she went into Hays' office to bring him up to speed.

"Are you going to come out with us, Mick?"

"No. I'll stay here and monitor things as they develop. Why don't you get Pascal Brosnan to sit outside the Roundstone station reading the paper, and he can let you know when Chapman drives past?" Hays said.

"Good idea. I'll call him now," Lyons said.

She wondered if Hays was staying well clear so that if it all went wrong, he would be nowhere near it, and she would take the blame. It was an unsettling thought.

* * *

The Ryanair flight arrived ten minutes ahead of schedule at Knock airport in the west of Ireland. The flight was almost full, much to the amazement of Peter Chapman. There was only one car hire desk at the airport, and he had to wait in line for two other passengers to get their cars before he was served. After a few minutes, he got to the top of the queue, handed over his driving license, passport and credit card and was given the keys to a brand-new silver Ford Fiesta. He didn't notice the plain clothes Garda sitting innocently opposite the car hire desk reading the morning paper.

When Chapman left the building to find his car, which was parked just opposite the terminal building, the Garda went to the desk and got the number and colour of the car that Chapman had been given from the agent. He phoned the details through to Inspector Lyons in Galway.

The Fiesta had a sat nav, which was handy, and before setting off Chapman input the details that would get him to Roundstone village. The device informed him that it would take him an hour and fifty minutes to arrive at his destination. He had spent the previous night studying maps of the area carefully. He had found the location that the Gardaí had sent him pretending to be Eddie Turner and saw that it was at the end of a very narrow track that led down to the coast, just off the N341 between Roundstone and Clifden. But instead of going directly there, he stopped in Roundstone outside O'Dowd's Bar near the harbour.

* * *

The detectives were in position by early afternoon. The weather was closing in, with the breeze strengthening, and ominous heavy grey clouds amassing in the west. But for the moment at least, the sun was still shining, although it had become noticeably cooler. They had been unable to secure the services of the Armed Response Unit at such short notice – the unit was otherwise occupied with a high priority assignment, and couldn't be diverted to assist them.

Fahy had picked up Joe Mason and Brutus as instructed, and the three of them were concealed in the old broken-down shed adjacent to the ruined cottage. Mason had instructed the dog to be silent, and it was clear that the dog understood the command, for he made not a sound. The tin roof on the shed had largely blown away in the wind, and the breeze whistled through the place, making it uncomfortable for them. The rest of the team were hidden at various points along the narrow cart track that led down from the road. The track forked here and there, affording access to the old famine homesteads that were now in ruin, or had disappeared altogether. The tiny houses had been constructed by placing rocks on top of one another by destitute families in the mid nineteenth century when the potato crop had failed, and they had moved to the coast in the hope of feeding themselves on fish and even seaweed. It had been a bleak time in Irish history.

While Sally Fahy and Joe Mason could hear nothing but the birds tweeting in the marshy ground surrounding them, Brutus suddenly pricked up his ears, whimpered quietly, and looked at Mason intently as if seeking instructions, but the Gardaí could still hear nothing.

A few minutes later, Brutus stood up and became quite agitated, again whining softly and almost begging his handler to come with him. The two Gardaí listened intently, but the sound of the wind blotted out almost everything, and they could decipher no noise of interest. Then, suddenly they heard the sound of rocks falling to the ground from inside the nearby ruin as Chapman retrieved the bag from the chimney of the old house.

"All units. All units. He's here. At the cottage. Hurry up, we need backup," Fahy shouted into her radio.

The three of them left their hiding place and sprinted towards the cottage. They were just in time to see the back of Peter Chapman running towards the sea clutching the red sports bag that Mulholland had left there previously.

They shouted at the fleeing form, "Stop, police, you're under arrest," but the fugitive took no notice and just kept running towards the shore. There, he hopped into a small open wooden boat, untied it from the rock it was moored on, and made off under the power of an outboard motor.

"Shit. He's got a boat. He's getting away," Sally Fahy screamed into the radio as Brutus scampered to the shoreline barking fiercely. He would have gone into the sea to try and swim to the little blue boat if Mason hadn't held him back with a taut lead.

Flynn and Lyons raced down the track to the shore, just in time to see Chapman disappear around a rocky outcrop, with the outboard motor on full throttle belching out a cloud of blue smoke.

"Shit, shit, shit. He must have guessed it was a trap. He's made us look like right eejits now, hasn't he?" Lyons said.

"Eamon, get onto Pascal. Get him to find out whose boat that is and where it came from. He must have a getaway plan," Lyons said.

Lyons then got on the phone to Mick Hays and told him what had happened. To say he wasn't best pleased would be an understatement. When Lyons had hung up, he thought about the situation for a moment, then lifted the phone.

"Hi, John, this is Mick. How's things?"

John Lambert was the coxswain of the Clifden lifeboat. He was also a member of the same sailing club as

Hays, and had often acted as crew when Hays had made longer forays out beyond the shelter of land in the Folkboat.

When Hays explained the situation, Lambert responded just as Hays had hoped he would.

"OK. We'll turn out. He's in an open boat, and the wind is freshening. He could be in danger. It'll take us about forty-five minutes to get around there. Have you a marine radio with you?" Lambert said.

"No. But I can get one of my folks out at the site to get hold of one. Inspector Lyons is leading out there," Hays said.

"Right. I'll get going now so, talk to you later," Lambert said, and as he finished the call, Hays could hear the whoop whoop of the alarm that would summon the crew of the lifeboat.

Ten minutes later, the lifeboat was launched with four crew on board. It headed out in a south westerly direction, across Mannin Bay towards Murvey. The sea was indeed getting up, and as they rounded the peninsula, slipping through between the many small islands, and on past Joyce's Sound, metre high waves crashed into the bow of the boat sending spray high into the air and over the bright orange superstructure.

Lyons had sent Sally Fahy off to get a portable marine radio, and twenty minutes later she returned to the spot where Chapman had tricked them armed with a fully charged Garmin marine portable.

"The man that gave it to me said the lifeboat will be on channel sixteen," Sally said, handing the radio to Lyons.

Lyons twisted the dial until the little red numbers on the display screen read '16'. She pressed the transmit button on the side of the unit, "Lyons to Clifden lifeboat, do you read me?"

Lambert came back at once, "Yes, Inspector, please switch to working channel forty-four, over."

When they had synchronized communications, Lambert said, "We are just coming around into Ballyconneely Bay now. Where do you think your man is headed? Over."

"Probably back towards Roundstone. That's where he hired the boat, over."

"It's getting pretty choppy out here for an open boat. If he doesn't know what he's doing, he could be in trouble. We'll head over in that direction and see what we can find. Keep this channel open, over."

"Roger, over," said Lyons, getting the hang of the jargon.

As she stood on the shore, Lyons could see the bright orange topside of the lifeboat ploughing its way across her view from right to left. The sea had gone an ugly green colour, and white horses were breaking on the tops of the waves which now crashed to the shore with an unwelcoming roar.

Ten minutes passed with no further word from the lifeboat, then Lambert was back on the radio.

"We have sight of a blue and white open boat about five minutes away further east. It appears to be drifting. It keeps disappearing in the troughs of the waves, over," Lambert said.

"That sounds like our man. Right colour of boat anyway. Call me when you're alongside, over."

A few minutes later, Lyons' radio crackled into life again.

"We're alongside now, Inspector. No sign of anyone on board, and the engine's not running. I'm going to put a man on the boat. We'll need to search for the person who was helming it. Over," Lambert said.

Lambert got one of his men on board the small boat. It was empty, except for a red sports bag and the fuel tank, which was completely dry.

"Looks like he ran out of fuel and started drifting out to sea. The current runs quite hard here, especially with the tide going out. He may have thought he could swim to shore. We'll go in close to the rocks, see if we can find him. I'll give Padraig some fuel for the boat, and we'll bring it back into Roundstone. Over," Lambert said.

"Thanks, John. We'll go and meet Padraig with the boat, there may be some forensics in it for us. Let me know if you find him. Over," Lyons said.

"Will do, over and out."

Padraig steered the little boat back towards the harbour at Roundstone. It was a difficult journey with the waves getting ever bigger and the small outboard engine struggling against the tide, but Padraig was well used to such situations, and it wasn't long before he rounded the harbour wall, his oilskins dripping with sea spray, much to the relief of its owner who had feared the worst.

"I told the beggar not to rev the engine hard. When you do that, it drinks fuel. No wonder he ran out. Any sign of him?" the weather-beaten old man asked.

"Not yet, but the lifeboat is still looking," Lyons said.

"Ah they'll not find him today. Once the sea has him, with the wind and the current out there, he'll be washed away. Ye'll get him tomorrow out by Gurteen, wait till you see. Poor beggar," the old man said.

The lifeboat stood down after searching without success for three hours. Lambert informed Lyons, and she thanked them for their help. Sally was sent off with Padraig to drive him back into Clifden and re-join the rest of the crew.

Chapter Twenty-five

Lyons and Fahy stayed out in Roundstone overnight. They booked into The Roundstone House Hotel, known for its excellent cuisine, and over dinner Maureen used the opportunity to probe the younger officer about her newly acquired career.

"How are you finding it – being a Detective Garda I mean?" Lyons said between courses.

"It's going well, for me anyway. I haven't had any negatives at all yet, and the team all seem really nice. I don't know if I'm doing any good though, it's hard to tell," the younger officer said.

"That's our fault, Sally. We should be providing more feedback. But you have fitted in so well, we kind of treat you as one of the guys. It's silly to make assumptions. I'll talk to Mick and see if we can't improve a bit. You're enjoying it anyway?" Lyons said.

"Oh yes. Of course there are some times when you'd rather be somewhere else, like when we have to deal with a bad road accident, or even on this case, when the boy was found dead in the boot of the car, but I'm learning to be more detached. I'll be fine," Fahy said.

"I know what you mean. Some of those things still get to me too, but you just have to stay objective. I know it's not easy. How's the love life?" Lyons said, changing the subject rather abruptly.

"Oh, you know. I've been going out with Kevin for nearly three months now. We get along grand, but he's not very exciting. We always do the same things – the pub, his place, sometimes a meal out at the weekend. He's kind though, I guess that's something," Fahy said.

"Something, but not enough. How is he in bed?"

"Jesus, boss, you'll be asking me for photographs next!"

Lyons raised her eyebrows in a questioning way.

"OK. Not that good to be honest. Like most guys, he's more interested in his own gratification than mine, and that's all I'm saying. What about you and Mick?" Fahy asked. She felt she had been given license to enquire as Lyons had been so forthright.

"It's going well. But sometimes I feel he still thinks of me as the junior officer, even at home. I know he has loads more experience than me, but I fought hard to get to where I am, and I'm not a bad cop."

"That's for sure. And you're tough too – look at that business with McFadden. Most Gardaí, never mind a woman, would have just surrendered to him," Fahy said.

"Not bloody likely, the little toe-rag. Anyway, I rather enjoyed bashing him in the nuts!"

They both laughed.

"And what about you and Mick in the sack?" Fahy went on shamelessly.

"That's great. We've always been good together. I just wish he would treat me more as his equal in work. That's really why I went for Inspector you know. I didn't want the higher post, but I felt as long as we were of equal rank, he'd have to treat me differently. But don't worry, I'm working on it."

Just then the waitress came with their next course and they tucked into the delicious food, tasting all the better as it was at the taxpayers' expense.

* * *

Just as the old timer had predicted, the body of Peter Chapman was washed up on the shore at the outer edge of Gurteen Bay the following morning. The body had been found by another old man who was out with his dog tending to a few scrawny sheep.

The wind had dropped and the sea was now calm, so Chapman's corpse made an incongruous sight lying twisted and bloated on the white sand, the waves gently tickling his feet.

Garda Pascal Brosnan found the two detectives at breakfast in the hotel as he sought them out to break the news.

"The old man was right," Lyons said.

"He was, to be sure. That man knows every inch of those waters personally, and unlike your man, he knows how to respect the sea," Brosnan said.

They didn't bother to get Dr Dodd out to the body. It was clear that he had drowned, so an ambulance was summoned to bring the body back into Galway where Dodd could perform the PM.

When Lyons called the doctor to tell him that it was on its way, he said, "Ah, that's better. A delivery service at last. Thank you, Inspector."

The detectives got back into Galway at midday. The mood was sombre. The case had been one big cock up from the start. There were three dead, and although they had two in custody, the main conspirator was one of the deceased. When Lyons walked dejectedly into Hays' office he said, "You look as if you have won the Lotto and lost the ticket."

"Ha ha, very funny. Jesus, Mick, this whole thing has been a major cluster fuck from the off. I can see me back on traffic duty before the weekend," she said.

"Not at all girl, don't be so maudlin. Plunkett's happy enough to have the whole thing cleared up. He's taken the view that the crime was really an English matter, just acted out on our turf, a bit like the Battle of the Boyne! And McFadden will go away for a good stretch, so it's not all bad," Hays said.

"After lunch we'll go and have another go at Eddie. With Chapman out of the way he'll tell us what's what to try and save his own neck, wait till you see," Hays said.

* * *

Eddie Turner was in a bad mood.

"You lot can't keep me locked up in here like this. I know my rights. I'll do you for false imprisonment – bloody Paddies," he ranted on.

Hays and Lyons let him vent. When he had exhausted the expletives, Hays cut in, "Right, Eddie. We thought we should bring you up to date with developments. This morning your partner in crime, Peter Chapman, was washed up on the shore out near Roundstone. It turns out he wasn't a seafaring man."

"That's nonsense. It's a trick. You'll not catch me out that easily," Turner said.

Lyons reached for her phone and loaded the photographs she had taken that morning out at Gurteen. She turned the phone around and held it up in front of Turner's face.

"No tricks, Eddie. Just another dead body for us to deal with," she said.

"Jesus Christ. How the hell did that happen?" Turner said, looking away quickly from the gruesome picture.

Lyons went on to explain the events that had led to the demise of Peter Chapman.

"That's not the first unsuspecting amateur the sea has taken out that way, and I dare say it won't be the last. The idiot didn't even have a life jacket," Hays said.

"So now, Eddie," he went on, "if you want to get out of here, it's time for you to tell us what's behind this whole ugly mess."

"What's in it for me?" Turner said.

"If you tell us all you know, Eddie, we'll see what we can do. No promises mind, let's see what you have first," Lyons said.

"OK. Well with Chapman dead, I should be able to hold onto all my fingers at least. You know old man Craigue used to work for Chapman's father in London back in the 1980s?" Turner said.

"Yes, he told us that," Lyons said.

"Well he left Chapman's firm and set up his own printing firm, kinda in competition see. Then, one by one, he picked off his old boss' customers by offering them cheap deals. Chapman's business went downhill, and after a while he had to turn to some dodgy stuff just to keep the place going," Turner said.

"What sort of dodgy stuff?" Hays said.

"Oh, you know, a bit of forgery here and there, labels, boxes for some of the boys up the West End that flog horse piss in Chanel No. 5 bottles, that sort of thing. Then he branched out into iffy tenners. They were good too – better than the real thing, some said. For a while he was the best in London, and he wasn't short of work. He used a team of runners to take the notes off to places like Benidorm and Majorca and change them in the foreign exchange shops, then bring the Pesetas back to the UK and swap them back for real money. At one stage he was clearing twenty grand a week," Turner said.

"Then his son Peter came into the business. Peter was a mad bastard. No fear. Thought he was invincible. He got in with a really bad crowd and before long they owned him. He wanted out. He was going to move to Spain, get away from the whole scene. Buy a little hacienda up in the hills somewhere, but he needed capital," Turner said.

"So, he thought Bernard Craigue would be a soft touch," Lyons said.

"He knew Craigue had sold his business for a good wedge. And he knew all about the lad, and the fact that they had bought a place out here. Anyway, he reckoned Craigue owed him for taking his father's business, so he asked me to help him set it up. No one was supposed to get hurt. All we was going to do was keep the boy in a rented house till we had the ransom and then let him go. Easy money, and Craigue wouldn't have even missed a hundred grand. I sussed out McFadden in Galway and he looked like a likely lad, and he had that good-looking chick with him – perfect. Pity I didn't know he couldn't drive proper," Turner said.

"And what were you going to get out of it?" Lyons said.

"Ten grand, and I had to give the driver and his girl a grand out of that," Turner said.

"So, what's going to happen to me now?" Turner said.

"We're going to talk to the superintendent, see what he wants to do with you," Hays said.

* * *

When Hays got back to his desk there was a message there for him to call Dr Julian Dodd.

"Can you deal with the good doctor, Maureen, I need to go and see Plunkett?" Hays said.

"Yeah, sure. I'll call him now."

"Well, Doc. Mick asked me to give you a call, he's with the superintendent," Lyons said.

"Ah, Inspector. It's just about the body you sent me in this morning. Very straightforward. Lungs full of the Atlantic Ocean I'm afraid. No unexpected marks or trauma – he was in pretty good shape till he went swimming. I'll keep him here till you can arrange something."

"OK, Doc, thanks."

* * *

Superintendent Plunkett was in a relatively good mood.

"Ah, Mick. Come in, take a seat. I hear you pulled another body out of the sea over this kidnapping thing."

"Yes, sir. The so-called brains behind the whole thing, if you could call it that," Hays said.

"Jaysus, Mick, this hasn't been our finest hour."

"No, but in fairness it wasn't really our fault," Hays said.

"No matter. The press won't see it that way. 'Dog's Dinner at Dog's Bay'" he said, drawing an imaginary headline with his fingers in the air. Hays smiled.

"Do you think you could tidy it up a bit, Mick? Play it down, make some of it go away," the superintendent said.

"I'm not sure, boss. The driver has already been processed, but we might be able to do something about the other clown, Turner."

"What have you in mind, or do I want to know?" Plunkett said.

"Nothing like that, boss. I was thinking the Brits might like to have him back. I got the impression they've been looking for him for a while anyway. They have a couple of warrants out for him."

"Excellent! But keep me out of it, won't ye? And do it quietly, no press. We're OK with the driver, that's a good story – North-South co-operation, hands across the border and all that bullshit, and if he gets Judge Meehan, he'll go down for a decent stretch," Plunkett said.

"Something tells me that's exactly what will happen." Hays said exchanging a knowing look with his superior officer.

"Ah, away with ye now. Oh, and Mick, how did Inspector Lyons do on this one?"

"She's not happy, but she did OK. She needs a few more straightforward cases to build up her confidence, but she knows I have her back," Hays said.

"Good man, Mick, that's the spirit."

* * *

A few minutes later, back at his desk, Hays called DCI Irene Russell in London.

"Afternoon Irene. How's things?" he said.

"Oh, just peachy as ever, Mick, and you?"

"Same. Look, we have this Eddie Turner guy here and we're not sure what to do with him. Is there any chance you'd like him back?" Hays said.

"Let's see, I'll just look him up on the system." The conversation paused while DCI Russell consulted the Met's computer.

"Hmm, well we have two warrants out for him, so it would be handy to have him back all right. We could close the file and get him banged up for a year or two," the DCI said.

"OK. But it has to be low key – no drama, and no publicity. I can get someone from here to fly over with him and hand him over at Heathrow. But just in arrivals, no squad cars on the tarmac. Is that OK?" Hays said.

"Sounds good. Call me when you have the flight details and I'll set it up this end. Thanks, Mick."

They didn't have much trouble convincing Eddie Turner that he would be better off in the UK. As they were explaining his options to him, mention was made of suspected subversive activity, and how some English prisoners get welcomed in Irish prisons. Of course the detectives talked it up a good bit, but Turner didn't know any better, so in the end he was happy to volunteer to fly back to the mainland and take his chances.

Chapter Twenty-six

Sally Fahy phoned Pat Bolger on the number his wife had given her. She arranged to meet him at the bar of the Imperial Hotel on Eyre Square at six o'clock, telling him that it was just a routine meeting to tie up some loose ends concerning the death of his step-daughter.

Bolger had been reluctant at first, but when Fahy offered to have the meeting at his home, Bolger quickly agreed to the hotel meet.

Fahy had filled Lyons in on the situation, and it was agreed that Detective Sergeant Eamon Flynn would go with Sally to the meeting, but that Sally would lead the interview.

Bolger turned up at five past six, got himself a pint, and sat down in a quiet corner with the two Gardaí.

"How can I help you?" he said.

"As you know Mr Bolger, your step-daughter Sheila was killed in a road traffic incident out near Roundstone the other day. That incident occurred during the execution of a failed kidnap in which Sheila was involved. We'd just like to ask you what you know of her acquaintances since she left home," Sally said.

"Nothing. Nothing at all. I haven't seen the girl since she ran away. Where was she living anyway?" Bolger said.

"We believe she was sleeping rough, Mr Bolger, but we're not sure exactly where."

"Oh, that's terrible. I wish I had known, I would have helped her out," he said.

"Can you tell us why it was that Sheila suddenly left her home, Mr Bolger? It seems strange to us that she would just up and leave for no good reason," Fahy asked.

"I've no idea. She didn't say anything – just left all of a sudden."

"Is that so?" Flynn interjected.

"Because we have a witness who says she left home because you were interfering with her," Flynn went on.

Bolger's face went red.

"That's nonsense. Who told you that? I'll sue the bugger! Damned lies!"

"You're lucky, Mr Bolger. The witness is not in a position to provide a statement, but he told us that he got it directly from Sheila, and he fully believed the poor girl who had nothing to gain from making up such a story," Flynn said. "And to be honest, if Sheila hadn't left home and got in with a bad crowd, she'd almost certainly be alive today, so you need to think about the consequences of your actions."

Bolger was about to speak, but Flynn put up his hand.

"Now I want you to listen very carefully to me, Mr Bolger. There's another wee girl living with Marie and yourself in that cosy little home you have out at Ardilaun. She's just starting to grow up, and frankly, we're a bit concerned about her safety. So, we'll be watching, Mr Bolger, and at the first sign, or any sign, that you are acting inappropriately towards her, she'll be taken into care under a place of safety order, and you'll be arrested. And we *will* know, Mr Bolger, trust me, we have our methods. You're on very thin ice here." Flynn said.

Bolger said nothing, and the detectives, having delivered their message, and having done as much as they could for now to protect Amy, got up to leave. As Sally Fahy turned to go, her coat caught on Bolger's almost full pint and sent it flying into his lap, soaking the front of his trousers.

"Oops!" she said, and walked out.

Chapter Twenty-seven

Detective Sergeant Eamon Flynn sat beside Eddie Turner on the Aer Lingus flight to Heathrow the following day. Turner seemed relieved to be getting out of Ireland, but not quite so pleased when he learned of the welcoming committee that awaited him in London. Still, it was better than being stuck in an Irish prison, he reckoned.

The flight went smoothly. DCI Russell had arranged for them to go through a priority channel for passport control, and a few minutes later, after a long walk, Flynn and Turner emerged into the arrivals hall.

A very young detective constable was there to meet them, with a piece of white card bearing the name Flynn in black marker held out in front of him. The young man introduced himself as John Stokes, and after a few pleasantries about the flight, Turner was duly handed over. As Stokes and Turner walked towards the exit, Eddie said, "Listen mate, I'm busting for a piss. That Irish fucker wouldn't let me go on the plane. Can we find a john?"

Stokes agreed, and they made their way across the concourse to the toilets. Turner made straight for the disabled one, went in and locked the door before Stokes could say anything. Feeling the need for relief himself, Stokes continued on into the gents, safe in the knowledge that Turner would be occupied for a few minutes at least.

Turner waited about ten seconds inside the disabled toilet, and then opened the door of the washroom gingerly. Great – no sign of Stokes. He slipped out of the toilet and walked briskly back to where lots of people were milling around, and simply disappeared into the crowd.

The Galway detectives never got to hear of Turner's escape. DCI Russell was too embarrassed to tell Hays what had happened. Turner had made good his getaway and would once again be sought by police forces all over the UK. What no one knew was that Turner had been paid up front by Chapman – not ten thousand, but twenty thousand pounds, with the promise of another ten thousand on successful completion of the job. Eddie had left a fake passport and a spare bank card in baggage storage at Heathrow, and before the police could circulate his details, he was away on an Iberia flight to Alicante.

Hays reported to Plunkett the following day that the 'loose end' had been taken care of. The superintendent was pleased, and asked that his thanks be passed on to the entire team.

Lyons wasn't happy. She felt that she had made a mess of the case, and if it hadn't been for Hays who had been there to dig her out, the whole thing might have gone very badly indeed.

Their last task before closing the file, was to visit the Craigues one last time at their house out in Ballyconneely.

A 'For Sale' sign had been erected in the front garden, with the sale being in the hands of a local estate agent from Clifden. Bernard Craigue was aghast to hear of the involvement of Peter Chapman. He was torn between anger and shame for how the kidnap and death of his only son had come about. His wife had become ill from it all, and in fact, never recovered.

List of Characters

Senior Detective Inspector Mick Hays – a keen sailor and the senior officer in the Galway Detective Unit, with many years' experience in crime detection. Hays is building a strong team in anticipation of an expansion of the unit in the near future.

Detective Inspector Maureen Lyons – Hays' 'bagman' in Galway, Maureen is constantly trying to prove herself while wrestling with self-doubt. A feisty, ambitious and tough woman with powerful instincts who has a knack of being in the right place at the right time.

Detective Sergeant Eamon Flynn – known for his tenacity, Flynn wanted to work as a detective since he was a small boy. He develops his skill while working on the case and proves invaluable handling some tricky customers.

Garda John O'Connor – the nerdy and modest junior member of the team is a technical wizard. He loves working with PCs, mobile phones, cameras and anything electronic.

Sergeant Séan Mulholland – happy to take it easy in the quiet backwater of Clifden, Mulholland could have retired by now, but enjoys the status that the job affords him. Not to be hurried, he runs the Garda Station at a gentle pace.

Garda Jim Dolan – works alongside Mulholland and has little ambition to do anything else.

Superintendent Finbarr Plunkett – a wily old character who is politically savvy, he manages the detective unit with subtlety. He's well-connected in Galway and exploits his connections to good effect.

Detective Garda Sally Fahy – the newest member of the team in Galway is still finding her feet but is already making an impression.

DCI Irene Russell – a highly experienced Metropolitan Police officer with a soft spot for Hays.

Dr Julian Dodd – an excellent pathologist with a rather superior air, who is always on hand to sort out dead bodies.

Sinéad Loughran – the forensics girl that manages to stay cheerful even in the most gruesome circumstances.

Joe Mason – the dog handler who manages Brutus, a beautiful and talented German Shepherd.

Garda Pascal Brosnan – runs the Garda station in Roundstone single-handed.

Lorcan McFadden – a small time crook from Galway with big ideas, but without the skills to match.

Sheila O'Rourke – a troubled teenager who had to leave home when her mother re-married.

Eddie Turner – an English criminal from London who finds himself out of his depth when dealing with the Irish police.

Bernard Craigue – a clever businessman who has done well at the expense of others, with a love of the west of Ireland.

Hannah Craigue – Bernard's long-suffering wife.

Jeremy Craigue – son of Bernard and Hannah who enjoys the night life in Clifden during the summer months and doesn't want to follow his father into the printing business.

Samuel Chapman – Bernard Craigue's ex-employer whose business has hit difficult times.

Peter Chapman – Samuel's son, a ne'er-do-well who finds himself all at sea.

Tadgh Deasy – a garage owner and mechanic that serves the people of Roundstone with all their motoring needs.

Shay Deasy – Tadgh's son.

Pat Bolger – believes he has found the perfect match with Marie O'Rourke and her two daughters.

Marie Bolger – mother of Sheila and Amy O'Rourke who re-marries with more haste than good judgement.

John Lambert – coxswain of the Clifden lifeboat, dedicated to saving lives at sea.

Padraig – a life boatman highly knowledgeable about the waters around Galway Bay.

Paddy McKeever – the rural postman who travels all over Connemara in his little green van.

If you enjoyed this book, please let others know by leaving a quick review on Amazon. Also, if you spot anything untoward in the paperback, get in touch. We strive for the best quality and appreciate reader feedback.

editor@thebookfolks.com

www.thebookfolks.com

BOOKS BY DAVID PEARSON

In this series:

Murder on the Old Bog Road (Book 1)
Murder at the Old Cottage (Book 2)
Murder on the West Coast (Book 3)
Murder at the Pony Show (Book 4)
Murder on Pay Day (Book 5)
Murder in the Air (Book 6)
Murder at the Holiday Home (Book 7)
Murder on the Peninsula (Book 8)
Murder at the Races (Book 9)

A woman is found in a ditch, murdered. As the list of suspects grows, an Irish town's dirty secrets are exposed. Detective Inspector Mick Hays and DS Maureen Lyons are called in to investigate. But getting the locals to even speak to the police will take some doing. Will they find the killer in their midst?

When a nurse finds a reclusive old man dead in his armchair in his tumbledown cottage, the local Garda surmise he was the victim of a burglary gone wrong. However, having suffered a violent death and there being no apparent robbery, Irish detectives Hays and Lyons are not so sure. With no apparent motive it will take all their wits and training to track down the killer.

A man is found dead during the annual Connemara Pony Show. Panic spreads through the event when it is discovered he was murdered. Detective Maureen Lyons leads the investigation. But questioning the local bigwigs involved ruffles feathers and the powers that be threaten to stonewall the inquiry.

Following a tip-off, Irish police lie in wait for a robbery. But the criminals cleverly evade their grasp. Meanwhile, a body is found beneath a cliff. DCI Mick Hays' chances of promotion will be blown unless he sorts out the mess.

After a wealthy businessman's plane crashes into bogland it is discovered the engine was tampered with. But who out of the three occupants was the intended target? DI Maureen Lyons leads the investigation, which points to shady dealings and an even darker crime.

A local businessman is questioned when a young woman is found dead in his property. His caginess makes him a prime suspect in what is now a murder inquiry. But with no clear motive and no evidence, detectives will have a hard task proving their case. They'll have to follow the money, even if it leads them into danger.

When a body is found in a car on a remote beach, detectives suspect foul play. Their investigation leads them to believe the death is connected to corruption in local government. But rather than have to hunt down the killer, he approaches them. With one idea in mind: revenge. Working out against whom and why will be key to stopping him in his tracks.

One of the highlights of Ireland's horseracing calendar is marred when a successful bookmaker is robbed and killed in the restrooms. DI Maureen Lyons investigates but is not banking on a troublemaker emerging from within the police ranks. Her team will have to deal with the shenanigans and catch a killer.

Made in the USA
Monee, IL
22 November 2019